Up and Away!

UP and AWAY!

Miriam Young

ILLUSTRATED BY SAM SAVITT

Harcourt, Brace and Company, New York

To Nancy, to Sister Joanne Francis, O.P., and to Mike Hines who made it all possible

Contents

Contents

Up and Away!

CHAPTER ONE

Boots and Bridles

A whole hour on a horse! Wendy Mason's hand closed excitedly on the baby-sitting money in her pocket. She could hardly believe it was really going to happen.

For over a year she had been reading horse stories and collecting china horses, but lately she had been yearning for something more active than that. She wanted to be around real horses, to see and touch and feed them and, most of all, to ride. And now in October, when fallen leaves lay like golden banners along the roadside, that wish was to be realized.

"Aren't you excited?" she asked the girl walking beside her.

Maureen O'Mara grinned, wrinkling her turned-up nose. "Well, I know one thing: I can't even breathe right."

"Me neither." Wendy laughed. "Oh, look!" She pointed to a hoofprint in the dirt road. "Soon *we'll* be making them!"

They hurried along, their sneakers sending up puffs of brown dust, until they had to slow down for lack of breath.

"A whole hour!" Wendy was exultant. "A whole half-hour each."

Maureen scowled. "If it wasn't for me, you'd have a whole hour for yourself."

"Dopey! That wouldn't be any fun," Wendy answered honestly.

As a matter of fact, without Maureen beside her Wendy would have been too shy to approach an elegant riding academy like Boots and Bridles. But Maureen was willing to go anywhere, to try anything.

Wendy had lived at Acorn Lake all of her life—nearly twelve years. Maureen, who was a year older, had been at the lake just six months, but as soon as the O'Maras had moved in, the girls had become friends. They did not go to the same school—Wendy went to the public school, Maureen to St. Mary's—but they rode the same bus, for both schools were in the same village. They lived just across the road from each other, and they played together after school. Most important of all, they were united in their love of horses. Both girls wanted to ride more than anything else in the world.

All autumn they had talked of nothing else—ever since they had seen a rider flying by on a golden-brown horse, jumping a stone wall as easily as a deer. They agreed that they simply had to find a way to ride. And now, at last, they were really on their way.

In just a few minutes, the girls assured each other, they would be galloping along the golden road, flying past the flaming trees, colored leaves swirling like confetti behind them.

"There it is!" Maureen spurted ahead.

Wendy hesitated. The stable was painted pale yellow with white trim, its cupola topped with a great gold weathervane in the shape of a running stallion. Faced with such elegance, Wendy felt doubtful.

"Wait, Maureen."

There were horses in the field beyond, and she would have preferred to watch them for a few minutes, but Maureen was marching straight toward the door.

"Wait?" she asked. "What for?"

"They might say, 'Run along; you're just children.' "

"Who cares? Anyway, there are kids on horses back there."

In a second field two children in riding habits could be seen trotting along a dirt ring worn in the grass. Maureen opened the stable door and walked in. Wendy followed. The light was dim after the strong sunlight, and they stood a moment, blinking.

"Yes, girls?" The man who appeared looked like someone they might see on television, Wendy thought. His ruddy face with its small, dark mustache seemed too young for the white hair that waved thickly from his forehead. He wore highly polished boots, tan breeches, a tweed jacket, and a Tattersall vest.

"We want a horse," Maureen blurted. "I mean, we want to hire a horse, both of us." She giggled with embarrassment. "To ride; one at a time."

The man smiled and picked up an appointment book from a desk at the wall. "I think that might be arranged. Are your parents with you?"

"No, we just came by ourselves," Wendy said shyly.

"I see. And when would you like to ride?"

"Right now!" she cried, forgetting her shyness. And Maureen added, "The sooner the better!"

The man raised one eyebrow. "As you are?" His glance took in their dungarees, sweaters, and sneakers. "It's customary to call up for a reservation. I'm not sure I have a horse available."

Wendy looked past him to the stalls. Some were empty, but farther back she could see several dark heads and manes. She took a deep breath. The very smell of the stable— a strong, sweetish mingling of hay and horseflesh, saddle soap, manure, and leather—was almost unbearably exciting.

A horse shook his halter. Another stamped and sneezed.

A shiver of anticipation went up her back. Imagine having not just one horse, but a whole stable of horses! Imagine knowing them all by name, having them for friends, being able to ride whichever you chose! Why, you'd be the happiest person in the world!

Wendy looked at the man to see if such happiness was visible, but he was frowning, tapping a pencil against his even, white teeth. "Well, girls, I'm afraid . . ." He was interrupted by the ringing of the telephone. "Colonel Kirby," he said, answering it.

Maureen and Wendy were impressed. They raised their eyebrows and exchanged smiles. *A colonel.* And then, as if drawn by a magnet, they found themselves moving toward the stalls. All the horses looked equally beautiful to Wendy. She had brought an apple for the one they would ride, but how would they ever choose?

"I'm sorry, girls," Colonel Kirby began, "but . . ."

"We've got the money," Maureen assured him. "That is, Wendy has."

Wendy took the dollar from her pocket and held it toward him. The Colonel glanced down but made no move to take it. Wendy blushed. The money was quite wrinkled. She smoothed it as best she could and offered it again. One corner of the Colonel's mouth lifted slightly as he looked at it, and Wendy, feeling as if she were offering something unworthy of his notice, a dried leaf or a toad, blushed still deeper, and her eyes filled with moisture.

"I'm afraid that's hardly enough," the man said at last. "I charge five dollars an hour."

"Five dollars an hour! Wow!" Maureen exclaimed. She turned to Wendy with a shrug. "I guess that lets *us* out."

The Colonel's refusal of her money had been humiliating, and Wendy wanted nothing so much as to get away, but another part of her could not give up the dream that had seemed so close to realization. "How much . . . I mean, how long *could* we ride for a dollar? Fifteen minutes? Each?"

The Colonel glanced outside and then at his watch. "How much riding have you done?"

"I've never done any," Maureen admitted. "But I know I can."

"Me, too," said Wendy. She could picture herself riding along as clearly as if it were something she had already seen on home movies.

"Then renting one of my horses is out of the question," the Colonel stated. "I don't allow inexperienced riders on my horses. No reputable stable would. It would be bad for the horse and dangerous for the rider. You girls get a little experience riding and then come back, and we'll see what we can do."

Maureen tilted her chin up stubbornly. "If no stable will let us ride until we're experienced, and we can't get experience until we ride, how the heck are we going to do it?"

Wendy regarded her friend with admiration for such logic, but the stable owner looked at her as if he thought her merely fresh.

"You can take lessons," he said. "Good afternoon." He turned away.

"Mr.—uh—Colonel," Wendy said persistently. "How much do lessons cost?"

"Eight dollars an hour." Seeing by their faces that this had been a blow, Colonel Kirby added, "A groom would take you through the preliminaries, but I myself would take you in hand later on."

They walked heavily toward the door. "Well, thanks," Wendy murmured.

"Yeah, thanks for nothing!" Maureen muttered when they were outside.

In the field beside the stable a woman was riding a brown horse. The girls watched as she took him over a low jump. A few moments later the Colonel joined her on his own mount, a gray reined in tightly so that his neck arched in a sharp curve.

"Come *on*," Maureen urged, pulling at Wendy's arm. "Who wants to watch him? Eight dollars! What does he think we are—millionaires?"

"Yeah," Wendy said, turning reluctantly from the field. "He can keep his old horses. I only wish . . ."

She was interrupted by the sound of hoofbeats behind them on the road. The girls stepped aside, and a beautiful chestnut gelding went by at a trot, his coat gleaming in the late afternoon sun, his full mane rising and falling in rhythm with his gait. The rider, a lanky boy of fifteen, posting easily, touched the brim of his black velvet hunting cap.

"Afternoon."

They caught a glimpse of bright blue eyes, cheeks red as apples, a long neck, and a prominent Adam's apple. The girls stuck out their tongues at his back.

"Lucky duck!" Wendy grumbled. "He got the best one!"

"Colonel's pet! Stuck up!" Maureen called out, although by now the rider was far out of hearing.

"Hey, you know what," Wendy said thoughtfully. "That horse looked like the one we saw this morning. Remember? The one that jumped the wall like he was flying over it? He had that same white mark down his face."

"Yes, but that was a man riding this morning. Hey, let's holler something when he rides back to Boots and Bridles."

"What?"

"I don't know. Maybe 'Hey, Mr. Rockefeller, where's your yacht?' "

They walked slowly now, picking late goldenrod from the road bank, pulling the blossoms off through their fingers. Then Wendy had an idea. "Let's walk into Plumbridge and get sodas. I'll treat."

"Okay."

But their hearts grew heavy as they walked back, for here, along Cricket Hill Road, almost every house had its own stable and a horse or two.

Wendy pointed out a large white house with long black shutters. "That's where Debby Wayne lives. She goes to private school and takes her horse with her, if you can believe it, and stables it there."

The next house, a quarter of a mile farther on, belonged to the Mergendorfs. A palomino was grazing in the field.

"Look at him!" Wendy exclaimed. "The color of coffee ice cream! And they've only got two *little* kids." It seemed to her that such a fine horse was wasted on small children. And now they passed Twin Willows Farm with its red clay tennis courts, its caretaker's cottage, and large stable. Wendy sighed. It seemed that everybody in Lewisboro had horses but them.

"I wish we could afford a horse of our own," Maureen said.

"We couldn't keep one, anyway. You can't keep anything but dogs or cats at Acorn Lake," Wendy informed her. "It's the rules."

Acorn Lake was not much larger than a good-sized pond, and the houses on the water were few. The rest ambled up the surrounding hills and were hidden in the woods, but all were modest homes with not more than a quarter of an acre of ground. The Masons' house was on the lake; the O'Maras', just across the road.

"Rules, rules, rules." Maureen sighed. "Every place you go —rules."

"No dogs allowed at the beach," Wendy chanted. "No one allowed in the clubhouse in wet bathing suits. No motor boats—the lake's too small. No horses! No nothing!"

Because of a mutually owned water supply, residents of Acorn Lake had formed a club and built a clubhouse and beach at the northern end of the lake. There were just such rules as Wendy mentioned, and more.

By now the girls had left the dirt road behind and were following the main road to Plumbridge, the small village where their schools were. For some distance there were no houses, for all the land belonged to Mr. Carter Holiday.

The main house of Holiday Farm was set like a castle, high on a hill, but the farm, with its kennels, greenhouse, and vegetable gardens, the employees' cottages and the stable and stableyard, was in plain sight, just off the main road. They passed Holiday Farm every day on the school bus, but today Wendy caught sight of something that made her head swivel around for a second look.

"Hey, Maureen! Isn't that the horse that just passed us with that boy on it?"

"It might be. Let's go see."

They stole up the gravel driveway. There was no one in sight. The horse turned his head curiously as they neared the yard and ambled toward them. The yard was enclosed by a stone wall. The girls climbed up on the gate for a better look. The horse's ears pricked forward, and Wendy caught her breath. At close range the animal was even more beautiful. His coat was a rich, gleaming chestnut. His eyes were large and intelligent-looking. His mane and tail were the same color as his coat, and a narrow streak of white blazed his face, ending in an arrow point at his forehead.

"It is!" she cried. "It's the same horse. Have you ever seen anything more beautiful?"

"Hey! Then he doesn't belong to the Colonel!"

Suddenly their hearts felt lighter than they had since leaving Boots and Bridles, and they laughed aloud.

CHAPTER TWO

Holiday Farm

Wendy held out her hand, offering the apple she had brought for the Colonel's horses to the big chestnut. His ears went back and then forward, and he bent his head to her hand. Just then a tall, thin, sharp-faced man came out of the stable. Wendy jumped, and the apple rolled to the ground.

The man nodded pleasantly, however. "Afternoon, ladies. It's a fine day."

He spoke with an Irish brogue, and the singing lilt in his speech raised his voice at the end of his words, making them more like a question than a statement.

"Yes, it is," Wendy said, looking to see whether the horse found the apple. He did.

"We just came to look at the horse," Maureen hurried to say.

"A cat can look at a king, eh? And King he is." The man smiled, and his piercing blue eyes, almost obscured by bushy eyebrows, were friendly. "He likes callers, King does. Especially when they come with a bit of a present," he said, winking at Wendy. "Come in, then, and have a good look."

He opened the gate, at the same time reprimanding the horse. "Back! Back, you! You're not going anywhere."

The girls bounded in so eagerly that the horse shied. Holding his halter, the man said, "Take it easy, now," to the animal, and to the girls, "Never run at a horse. You'll frighten him."

They moved more slowly to stroke the horse's head and neck.

"Is that his name—King?" Maureen asked.

"King Donegal he's called. And he's king of the stable. He's been here the longest and considers the others interlopers."

"How many horses do you have?" Wendy asked.

"Five, in all, the boss has. But there are six stalls, and I hope to fill the empty one with a horse of my own someday."

As the girls continued to pat the horse and call him by name and to rub their noses against his silky neck, the man told them of a horse he had tried to buy from a man in Wilton, Connecticut.

" 'A thousand? You're out of your head, man,' I said. 'It's not a penny too much for a horse like this one,' he said, 'and well you know it, Timothy Doyle,' he said."

The girls scarcely listened. They were too absorbed in King Donegal. Besides, it was hard to understand the man's brogue. But suddenly they realized he was asking Maureen a question.

"Didn't I see you at the church in Plumbridge last Sunday?"

"We always go there except when we oversleep, and then we go to late Mass up at Croton Springs," she replied.

"I knew it! I knew I'd seen you someplace. I never forget a face, especially an Irish face like yours. With your parents, weren't you? Your mother's a tall, fine-looking woman, and your father a jolly-looking, chubby man?"

"Fat." Maureen smiled as she corrected him.

"Well, now," the man said diplomatically, "a bit of flesh is not bad on a man. Makes him look healthy. I'm a regular Jack Spratt myself. Barely enough flesh to cover my bones, my wife says, and eighteen of them broken."

"Eighteen?" Wendy exclaimed. "You've broken eighteen bones?"

"Eighteen it is, not counting little ones that mend themselves. It's part of the trade. If you meet a professional horse-man and he tells you he's never broken a bone, you may be sure you've met a liar."

"How did it happen? Were you thrown?"

"Thrown, yes. Rolled on, stepped on, tossed over fences. Knocked about and backed against stone walls. I've ridden many a mean horse in my time. The last man I worked for, Mr. Emmet Phillips of Westport, he bought one as vicious as they come. Sold on him, he was, but I could recognize that mean look in his eye a mile away."

"Where?" Maureen was patting King and not listening carefully. "I don't see any mean look."

"Not King, girl!" the man boomed, slapping the horse affectionately. "King has spirit, but he's no meaner than your baby brother."

"Well, *he* can be mean, sometimes," Maureen said, thinking of her six-year-old brother, Johnny.

The groom gave a shout of laughter. He then asked the girls where they lived and why they had come to see the horse. "I bet you wanted a ride on him, was that it?"

They exchanged wildly hopeful glances. Timothy Doyle nodded. "I can see you're real riders, the pair of you. You've the look of true horsewomen."

Their dreams collapsed. Their smiles faded. "We've never been on a horse, either of us," Wendy stated flatly.

There was a pause. Then the man said, "Well, you're honest, I'll say that for you. And you've a big advantage," he added, seeing their saddened faces. "Those who think they can ride and can't, them you can't reach a thing; but those who admit they can't ride, they can always learn."

"Yes, if they've got eight dollars for a lesson," Maureen muttered.

"Eight dollars!" Mr. Doyle's mouth dropped open, and he

fell back against the wall in exaggerated horror. "Holy saints! What robber is asking that much of children?"

The girls told him of their visit to Boots and Bridles.

"The pirate!" he exclaimed. "And what does the man know about riding, himself? Didn't I see him take a tumble at the hunter trials last week on a mare a baby of five could have handled? Took a beaut of a fall, he did. And doesn't he hold that gray of his so tight it's a wonder the poor beast has a mouth left on him at all!"

The girls were feeling more cheerful every moment. Wendy had heard that Colonel Kirby had ridden in the National Horse Show at Madison Square Garden and was an excellent horseman. But if Timothy Doyle said so, she was willing to believe the Colonel knew less about riding than Maureen's brother Johnny.

"It's a lucky thing you didn't have the money," Tim Doyle continued. "You'd be throwing it away. I'd hate to see you get your start, anyway, on those four-legged turkeys he calls horses. Why, I never saw such a bunch of slab-sided, cow-hocked, ewe-necked, mule-headed, sway-backed creatures in my life! Highway robbery that's what it is!"

He walked to the wall and started stretching out a cooling sheet to dry in the sun. "Here, girls, give me a hand. Take the other side, would you?" When it was stretched, he said, "Wait a bit, there are two more inside. Say, maybe you'd like a look at the other horses?"

Would they? They almost knocked him down running to the stable.

"Easy now. What are your names?" he asked, catching up with them.

"Maureen O'Mara."

"Mine's Wendy. Wendy Mason."

"Wendy, is it? That's a new one to me." He smiled at

Maureen. "My sister was called Maura. Same name, you know. Maureen means little Maura."

He held the stable door open for them. On their left a door led to the tack room; the one on the right led to the cow barn. Straight ahead were the stalls. The first was empty. It belonged to King, he told them. In the second they saw a beautiful black mare. Her dark coat gleamed like satin, black all over except for a drop of white, the size of a quarter, on her forehead.

"What do you say of her? Is that a fine mare or isn't it?"

"Is she queen of the stable?" Maureen asked, smiling.

"What? Queen? I suppose so. Her name is Latest Vogue. Vogue, around the stable. She's the one I ride myself, when we go hunting. The boss rides old King. He's a big man, Mr. Holiday, broad-shouldered and heavy; he needs a strong mount. Vogue, here, is half a hand taller, but King's a mite heavier."

In an opposite stall stood a young roan. This was Captain Dan, Mr. Doyle told them, a two-year-old and a newcomer to the stable.

"He's the prince, then." Maureen grinned.

The man scowled. "Knave is more like it. He's a bad actor, that one. Keep your distance."

In spite of the warning Maureen reached out a hand to stroke the roan. "He's nice. I like him."

"You won't think him nice if he takes a nip at you. We bought him for his lines. Great conformation, hasn't he? I'd have bought him myself if I'd had the money, for, properly trained, this horse will make a fine hunter. I had a time convincing the boss of it, though. He had his heart set on a mare belonging to Huntley Forbes—Rocket. 'Don't buy her,' I said, 'I don't like her looks.' And yet, next thing you know, here's Haggerty, Forbes's groom, with the van. 'What've you got there, Ed?' I ask him. 'You're not trying to palm off that goose-rumped, bull-necked, calf-kneed mare on us, now?' 'See here, Tim,' he says . . ."

Maureen went into the stall and pulled straw out of Vogue's mane. She was paying no more attention than was Wendy, who was running her hand down the black mare's silky neck. "Vogue, you look just like Black Beauty," Wendy said to the mare, who towered majestically above her.

" 'Now you listen to me, Haggerty,' I said," Tim Doyle continued, " 'I'm not risking the few sound bones I've got left training a mare with such poor conformation as that one. You can take your Rocket and shoot her off at Cape Canaveral,' I told him . . ."

Tim Doyle picked up two more blankets and carried them outside, and with the girls' help spread them to dry, talking all the while and using words they had never heard, such as snaffle, Pelham, pastern, cannon, and fetlock.

It seemed to Wendy that his brogue was thicker now and harder to understand; she gave up trying and began to daydream. . . . Vogue and Dan belonged to her and Maureen and they would ride to school, and all the other children would crowd around and ask for rides. . . .

She was startled out of her dream by a strong finger prodding her shoulder. "Eh, now?" Tim Doyle was asking. "Isn't that so?"

Wendy swallowed and was silent.

"You know what I can't stand?" he asked. "A person who doesn't listen when you talk. There was a woman here yesterday, came to ask about the pups. Mrs. Holiday raises these prize poodles, you know. Well, the kennelman being away, I told her what I could, throwing in a few little anecdotes to make it interesting. And can you beat it? The woman didn't hear a thing I said! I could tell by her face!"

Wendy took a deep breath and vowed silently to concentrate.

"But you two," Tim said, "you're well brought up. You listen. It's only mannerly. You heard every word I said now, didn't you?"

The girls looked at each other hopelessly, and Maureen answered with an indefinite "Mmm."

"What did I say, then?"

"You mean *everything?*" Maureen demanded.

"No, just what I said before, about choosing a horse. Remember? I said there were four things to look for in a hunter, especially if you're going to enter him in a three-day event. First: *conformation.* Long, sloping shoulders, a deep chest, a short back. Second: *stamina.* The guts to stand up to the strain of the hurdles. Third: *courage* to face what's before him—a grueling test. Fourth: the *intelligence* to take orders from his master. And last but most important, *experience.*"

That was five things, Wendy noticed, and Maureen began, "That's . . ." but stopped when Wendy nudged her.

"So! Four important points. Remember them. Well," the groom said, taking hold of King's halter and leading him toward the stable, "I've got to get King bedded down and then go after the ponies. I can't stand around socializing all day. You've made me late as it is. My wife will raise the devil if I'm late to supper."

"*We've* made *you* . . . !" Maureen's indignant outburst was halted by another nudge.

Timothy Doyle opened the stable door and bade them good-by. "Say," he called over his shoulder, "you don't happen to know a couple of boys, do you, who would be sensible and steady and not afraid to work? I could use a pair of stable hands. And I'd pay them by teaching them to ride."

Wendy and Maureen looked at each other with one thought.

"Sure!" Maureen grinned. "I know a couple of kids who'd make swell stableboys." And this time it was she who nudged Wendy. Wendy's blue eyes were brimming with laughter. She did not trust herself to speak.

"Send them round, then. Tell them to get permission from their parents. And mind you close that gate behind you."

He was no sooner out of sight than the girls fell into each other's arms, shrieking with joyous laughter. They ran down the gravel driveway, shouting and giggling with excitement. They danced all the way to Cricket Hill Road. There Maureen put her hands to her mouth and called out, "Ha-ha, Colonel Kirby! Ha! Ha! Ha!"

CHAPTER THREE

Stableboys

Wendy awoke feeling that the day held some special promise, but she could not think *what*. She jumped out of bed quickly to beat her brothers to the bathroom and was back getting dressed in another minute.

"Mom, can I wear dungarees to school today?" she called, already half into them.

Her mother usually agreed to all requests with a qualifying "if." "Yes," she would say, "if you're careful," or "Yes, if you don't stay too late," or "Yes, if your homework is done." This time she answered, "Yes, if you wear a nice, fresh blouse."

Wendy put on a blouse with blue embroidery that matched her eyes and, grabbing a brush and two elastic bands from her dresser, started down the stairs. A mist rising from the far side of the lake, seen through the dining room's bay window, told her the air was cool, and leaves floating like little boats near shore that the night had been windy.

She ate her egg and, with a stealthy look at her father, slipped the fatty part of her bacon from her plate. Mr. Mason was busy with the paper, and Patches, who lay under the table awaiting such treats, put his nose into Wendy's lap and was rewarded.

Steven, her fourteen-year-old brother, came thundering down the stairs.

"Holy smoke! You look like a witch!"

Wendy tossed her hair back from her face.

"That's worse! Now you look like an *ugly* witch!"

"Steven!" Mrs. Mason said reprovingly. "Stop teasing."

"*Teasing?* I *mean* it. She does."

Wendy wrinkled her short nose and cackled like the witch in *Snow White*. "Heh, heh, heh. Come try this lovely poisoned apple, my child."

Mrs. Mason drew Wendy away from the table and started brushing her hair, as eight-year-old Jamie put in an appearance.

"Ouch! I wish I had hair like Maureen's," Wendy complained.

"Don't be silly. Your hair is a lovely color. Halfway between brown and blond. I love it." Her mother made two little braids at the temple and caught these into two larger ones.

"I mean short, and naturally curly. All Maureen has to do is wash it and it's fixed."

"She must have that new Wash-and-Wear hair," her father suggested, as he folded the paper and rose to leave for the train to New York.

"Pigtails are such a bother," Wendy grumbled.

"Pigtails are for pigs," Jamie sang, and looked hopefully at Steven.

Steven paid no attention to the younger boy. He looked after Wendy as she dashed up the stairs. "Hey, you forgot something: your *broom*. Aren't you going to ride today?"

Wendy's face lit up joyfully. That was it! That was why the day was special. She was going to ride!

School seemed unusually long that day, but every so often Wendy would picture the groom's surprise on seeing his new "stableboys," and her eyes would light up again.

"I can't wait!" she said to Maureen, as they raced toward Holiday Farm after school. "Imagine his face when he sees it's *us!*"

Timothy Doyle, however, showed no surprise at all upon seeing the girls. He nodded in a matter-of-fact way and went on with his work, not even speaking except to say, "Stand back a bit, there's the girl," or "Out of the way, *if* you please."

"Can we do something to help?" Wendy ventured to ask after a few moments.

Tim Doyle spoke over his shoulder as he carried water to Dan's stall. "*Can* you? That's the question. Can you scrape down a horse that's just in from the hunt? Can you mix bran mash? Can you clean tack?"

He carried a pail of water to the rack at the front of the stable and began cleaning one of the two saddles resting upon it, grumbling all the while about the worthlessness of a pair of females who didn't know one end of a horse from the other.

"Well, the boys wouldn't have known any more than we do!" Maureen said, bristling.

"Boys? Who said anything about boys?"

"You did. You asked if we knew any who would work here."

"So we thought we'd surprise you and come ourselves," Wendy said.

"Surprise, eh?" He rubbed a sponge over a can of saddle soap. "After the way you two went off in a fit of giggles? I wasn't born yesterday, you know." He worked for a while. "Oh, you're no sillier than other girls, I suppose, but what I need is experienced helpers."

There it was again—that word. Maureen gave a snort of exasperation. "Will you tell me how the heck you *get* experience?"

"By working, girl. How do you think?"

Maureen set her lips in a determined line. Seeing another sponge, she dipped it into the water and saddle soap and began on the other saddle.

"For the love of the saints!" the groom cried. "What do you think you're doing?"

"Just what you're doing. Working."

He took the sponge from her. "Never do that. Never use a water sponge for soap, nor vice versa. Go on, now, go home. You're in my way."

Timothy Doyle was tired. He was always tired after hunting, and he and Mr. Holiday hunted every other day from October first to February. He had been up at dawn, getting the horses ready, had ridden to the meet at seven, and had followed the hounds with his employer until two. Then he had ridden home, looked the horses over for cuts and bruises, and had given them hay and water before going to the cottage for his own lunch.

At three he had returned to the stable to brush the dried mud from the horses and to clean the tack and the stalls. He turned wearily to the girls. They had not moved. "Well, what are you waiting for?"

Wendy's eyes had a shiny look, as if she thought by opening them wider and wider she could keep from crying with disappointment. Maureen's were snapping with anger. "Everybody says, 'Get experience,'" she protested. "But how can you get it if nobody will let you learn?"

Tim nodded. "I expect you're right. Well, if you must, you can hang around and watch. You might be of some use, I suppose."

They stood silent as he finished his work. Scowling and taciturn, he seemed a different person from the friendly, talkative man of the day before. But suddenly he surprised them by asking, "How'd you like to go after the ponies with me?"

They walked through the stable yard, out the back gate, and past a cottage he identified as his own. Like the other farm buildings—barn and stable and the homes of the other farm employees—it was white with blue shutters and trim. Left of the cottage a narrow road, rutted by truck tires, wound past an old carriage house in which a station wagon, a tractor, a small truck, and a power mower were stored. They walked over a hill and down through a wooded area, coming at last upon an open field.

There the girls gaped with surprise. "Are those the *ponies?*"

Wendy had expected to see the toy-sized burros she had seen at the Danbury Fair. These looked like horses. One, a bay with black mane, tail, and points, was as beautiful as an illustration in a book. The other, smaller and stockier, was a light chestnut with lighter mane and tail and a wide blaze of white down his face.

"They're ponies, all right," Tim answered. "Though if Lady had another quarter inch she'd be considered a horse. She's exactly fourteen-and-a-half hands; over fourteen-and-a-half is a horse."

"Gee, they're neat," Maureen said approvingly.

"Her name is Lady?" Wendy had fallen in love with the beautiful little bay at first sight.

Tim stroked the mare affectionately. "A perfect lady, and a perfect lady's mount. A calm disposition—a bit too calm, perhaps—but perfect conformation and perfect manners. You'd look far to find another pony as good."

The other pony came forward cautiously, ears flicking forward and back. Tim gave him a friendly slap on the rump. "And what do you think of this specimen of horseflesh? Good lines, would you say? Think he'd win a prize at a beauty parade?"

"Yes!" Wendy turned her admiration from the beautiful bay to the smaller pony. "He's darling!"

Tim snorted in disgust. "You'd never make a judge at a horse show, that's certain! Look at him! Short neck, big head . . ."

Stroking the pony, Wendy felt a scar. "Was he hurt?"

"That's a brand, my girl. Little Joe is a cow pony from the West."

Maureen wanted to know why Mr. Holiday had bought him, if he had so many faults.

"He's a good steady little fellow, and they wanted a sturdy animal for young Carter. Teddy, they call him."

Maureen's eyes flickered with interest. "Was he riding King yesterday?"

"Teddy on King!" Tim laughed. "Holy hat, but he'd roll right off! And never feel it. Sixty-five pounds of baby fat, that's Teddy. He's a bit young for riding at six. But Little Joe is not ready for him, either. That's another job I've got—getting the ponies in shape for the Holiday kids."

Wendy and Maureen exchanged hopeful glances, thinking this might be a job they could take off the groom's hands. And probably this is what Tim Doyle had in mind, for as they returned to the stable yard, leading the ponies, he told them that if they really wanted to work at the stable, they could start by picking up the ponies' stalls.

"But you'll be no use to me, mind, if you come only when you're in the mood. Stable work goes on day after day, and it's steady help I need, not intermittent."

And then, declaring it was more work showing them how than doing the work himself, he gave them each a basket and pitchfork and explained how the stalls must be cleaned.

They followed his directions as well as they could, but the straw that littered the floor when they were through brought a muttered complaint from the groom. "I knew it! Just makes more work for me."

Maureen, a line between her brows, and her lips set in a determined line, picked up the stable broom and swept the floor. "There! Does that suit your majesty?"

Tim gave her a sharp look. "Mind your manners, or you'll be sent packing. And what about you?" he asked Wendy. "Can't you carry a bucket? Are you weak, girl?" But when the work was done, the stalls spread with fresh straw, the horses watered and fed, Tim placed a wooden chair that had lost its back at the door and took a magazine called *The Chronicle* from a shelf.

"Well, now." He smiled, settling down to read. "I know you're aching to ride, so get on with it."

The ponies had been left in the yard. The girls tumbled past him, remembering in time not to run. Maureen, bigger and faster, was the first to reach Lady. Wendy stood beside the cow pony, wondering how to get on; neither pony was saddled.

"No! No!" She turned to see the groom whack Maureen with his magazine. "Never try to mount from that side! Don't you know that? Oh, Jupiter, what a green pair you are! And I thought I'd have a minute to rest. Here, you'd better go one at a time."

He came to Wendy and bent down, his fingers locked to form a basket. "You—Wednesday, or Thursday, or whatever it is—I'll give you a leg up."

"What?"

"Oh, for Pete's sake! Put your knee in here!"

Her knee had barely touched his hand, when she found herself upon the pony's back. Her heart gave a leap. It was much higher than she had expected. The pony felt bigger than he looked. Tim snapped a lead line to the halter and handed it to Maureen.

"Here, walk your friend around the yard; then it will be your turn."

For half an hour they led each other, never going faster than a walk. Still, it was a beginning. . . .

For the next two weeks they showed up every day. It was November now, and the trees were bare as broomsticks. Walking to the stable, the girls could see houses that had been hidden by October's brilliant foliage. They could even see the roof of the Holidays' big house, which, Tim said, had been brought from a castle in France, slate by slate. And one day, as they approached the farm, they saw a long black Cadillac parked by the stable and a man in riding clothes talking to the groom.

Tim made the introductions as the girls came into the yard.

"They may not look it, Mr. Holiday, but these two are my stableboys. I'm hoping they'll be some help in training the ponies for Master Teddy and Miss Barbara."

Mr. Holiday smiled at them. He was a big man, and broad-shouldered, but not as tall as the six-foot-three groom. "Well, isn't that . . ."

"That is," Tim interrupted, "*if* they behave themselves. *If* they stick. I'm forever being pestered by kids coming around wanting to ride. 'Teach us to ride?' " Tim mimicked them in falsetto. " 'Please, can we ride your horses?' But none of them wants to work for it. No."

"I think these two will stick," Mr. Holiday replied, giving the girls another smile. He waved his riding crop. "Well, so long, Tim."

Wendy wanted to thank Mr. Holiday for letting them ride his ponies, but before she could summon up the courage to

speak, he was gone, and she could only resolve to live up to his expectations and "stick."

Stick they did. They came to the stable to work every day including Saturdays and Sundays. Tim could count on them to clean the stalls and the tack and to listen when he talked.

"You won't find tack like this in every stable," he told them as they worked cleaning the bridles. "There's some I could name, not far from here, either, where the leather's so neglected it's stiff as lead pipe. No, you won't find reins as soft and pliable everywhere—not even in your fancy riding academies."

"Is that all we're ever going to do!" Maureen complained one day, when the groom had gone to his cottage while they worked. "Learn to clean tack?" The girls no longer led each other around, but they were still merely walking the ponies in the yard. "If he doesn't let us ride outside somewhere, or do something more exciting than just walk, I'm going to quit! I'm sore!"

Wendy was sore, too. Literally. The insides of her thighs were chafed and red from the ponies' rough coats, her calves ached, and her hands were blistered. And she yearned to do some real riding. But if Maureen rebelled, Mr. Doyle might become angry and send them home. He became angry quite easily, especially with Maureen.

"Maureen, you wouldn't just quit!"

"Wouldn't I? I want to trot, and I want a saddle. This riding bareback is for the birds!"

Wendy held her breath when Maureen stalked up to Tim as he came down the stone steps of the cottage. His answer surprised her. "Why, sure, girl. Trot if you want to. What's stopping you?"

Maureen led Lady to the backless chair and mounted. She

clicked her tongue, but Lady continued to amble slowly. "How do you get her to do it?"

"Put your heels into her sides. Show her you mean business."

She did so, and Lady went into a neat little trot. Maureen, however, bounced on her back like a ping-pong ball. Wendy watched in surprise. Why was Maureen jouncing like that? She got onto Little Joe's back and dug in her heels, and the next thing she knew, she was bumping along in the same way, her teeth knocking together. It was all she could do to hang on.

"Post! Post!" Tim called. "Don't just sit there like a sack of meal!"

"How?" Wendy managed to ask.

"Use your leg muscles. Get your knees up and pressed in. Nobody can teach you to post; you've got to get the feel of it. Get into the natural rhythm of the horse. Lady has a nice, easy rhythm. Anybody ought to be able to post on her. Well, keep trying. You'll get it."

"When can we ride with saddles?" Maureen asked.

"When you can post bareback—not before," he answered. "Come on, let's get the ponies to bed. They've had a hard day —two green jocks jouncing the divil out of their backs."

Wendy was glad to dismount. Tomorrow—she was sure— she would be able to post. They were really riding—practically.

CHAPTER FOUR

The Lanky Boy

Wendy sat, chin in hands, elbows on her school desk, her mind far from English composition. Posting looked so simple. She could see herself trotting as well as that lanky boy who had passed them on King that day in October, when she and Maureen had first decided to ride. Had that really been King, she wondered, or just a horse who looked exactly like him? And who was the tall, thin, freckled boy?

"Wendy Mason!" A voice interrupted her reverie. "That's the third time that's happened today! You may remain after school and explain your inattention."

"After school? Today? Oh, I can't today!" If she missed the first bus, Maureen would wonder where she was. And Mr. Doyle would think she was neglecting her work. "I can't today. I've got to go somewhere."

The teacher waited. "Yes?"

"To the dentist." Wendy had not planned to tell the lie. It just popped out.

"Very well, you may stay tomorrow instead."

"Oh, but tomorrow's just as bad! I mean . . ."

"You mean you have a dentist appointment tomorrow as well?" the teacher asked, and the class laughed at Wendy's discomfort. "I suggest," the teacher continued, "that you go to the principal's office now and confirm your dentist appointment. You don't seem to know which day it is. And if it is not for today, I would like you to stay and write me an explanation."

The first buses left the Lewisboro school. Wendy sat staring at a blank paper, wondering how to begin. She hated writing compositions, and now she had this one to write as well as the regular assignment. If only she could just *tell* Miss Allen how she had promised to work regularly at the stable, without missing a day! If only she could explain how important it was to "stick." At last she decided to do just that—to write it all in a letter, exactly as if she were speaking. And the words came easily. She was still writing, in fact, when the second bell rang and Miss Allen said, "That's enough now, Wendy. You may go."

Half an hour later she was knocking at the O'Maras' back door. She could hear a piano; Mrs. O'Mara gave music lessons. At her second knock little Johnny O'Mara appeared.

"I've got a snapper." He opened his hand just a little to show her.

"That's not a snapper; that's a plain baby turtle. Is Maureen here?"

"It is so a snapper! I heard it go *snap!*"

His mother came to the door. "Maureen left for the stable long ago. Where were you?"

Wendy admitted she had been kept after school. Mrs. O'Mara smiled and shook her head. "And I thought you were such an angel child! Now I feel better about *my* two. Johnny here is probably going to flunk out of kindergarten!"

"I go to school," Johnny called as Wendy ran down the steps. "I'm in Grade A."

"You're a Grade A rascal." Mrs. O'Mara scooped him up and gave him a spank. "Better hurry, Wendy; you'll lose your job."

Wendy ran nearly all the way to the farm. She was

pounding up the driveway when she heard the even beat of Lady's hoofs and saw, above the yard wall, Maureen's head and shoulders rise and lower evenly. Could Maureen *post?*

"Might as well go home" was Tim's greeting. "Work's all done; no point in your staying." But as Wendy's mouth drooped with disappointment, Tim's eyes crinkled beneath the straw-colored brows. "All right. Get the pony."

She climbed upon Little Joe's back, dug in her heels, pressed her thighs in close, and he went into a trot. For a while she bounced as she had the day before. Then suddenly— and briefly—she had it! She rose an inch or two and came down, as he trotted evenly around the yard, touched his back, rose again, and came down without a bounce. She looked back to see if Maureen and Tim were watching. At that moment she lost the rhythm and went bouncing along like a puppet on a string and did not post again.

Maureen, too, had apparently caught the trick of posting only briefly, but when they had dismounted, she turned to Wendy in triumph.

"Hey, I got it! Did you see me posting? I'll bet we could do it if we had saddles. I'm going to ask him tomorrow."

"Hey, Mom!" Wendy cried exultantly, tearing into the kitchen at suppertime. "Guess what: we can almost post! I *did* post for a few minutes!"

"That's fine, but do go up and take a bath."

"I just took one!" The ends of Wendy's pigtails were still wet.

"It must be getting into your skin then." Mrs. Mason often complained that the house smelled just like a stable. But what was wrong with that, Wendy wondered. A stable had a wonderful smell!

"Daddy," she said at the table, "Mr. Doyle says that as soon as we can post bareback, he's going to teach Maureen and I to . . ."

"Maureen and *me*." He corrected her wearily. "He's going to teach Maureen and *me*."

"No fooling, Dad?" Steven asked. "I didn't know *you* wanted to ride."

Wendy glared at her brother. "*Anyway*, he's going to teach us to canter and jump and everything."

"By the way," Steven asked casually, "what's it like in Dr. Low's office? I saw you heading in there today. Is it nice? Good view? Wall-to-wall books?"

Wendy paused, her fork halfway to her mouth. She had forgotten that she had been sent to the principal's office. And Jamie became interested in the conversation for the first time.

"Did you get sent to the principal's office? What did you *do?*"

"Nothing. I was—inattentive."

"Is that all?" her father asked. Mr. Mason, an assistant professor of English at New York University, was often absentminded himself.

"No, I—I told a lie. But I didn't mean to."

Wendy waited during the pause that followed this revelation. She had never been sent to the principal's office before and did not know what her parents' reaction would be. Would there be further punishment at home?

"I really didn't mean to," she protested. "I was thinking about riding, and it just popped out."

"I'm glad you have this opportunity to learn to ride," Mr. Mason said, "but if it's going to make you delinquent in your studies . . ."

"Gosh!" Jamie exclaimed. "Is Wendy a juvenile delinquent?"

"Don't talk with your mouth full," his mother said. "And let's say no more about it. At least, at the table."

"Boy, if *I* got caught in a lie and sent to Dr. Low's, I'd hear about it!" Steven complained.

Mr. Mason changed the subject. Dinner over, Wendy went to her room and waited. If they were going to scold her, she wished they would come and get it over with. She opened her books. In the living room the boys, having finished their homework in the afternoon, were watching television.

My name's Rick Kent. I'm out to get the man who killed my brother.

Wendy sighed. She had not been to the movies or seen television since she and Maureen had started working at the stable. It was fun, but it was not easy. And she never knew when Tim was going to yell at them. She struggled through her arithmetic. Jamie was sent to bed, and Steven tuned in a second program.

I'm on to you! You're trying to get the mine. But my father left me that mine. . . . And he left me this gun, too!

Mr. Mason came into Wendy's room. "How are you getting along? That program bother you?"

"No, I don't really hear it."

"I'm sorry about that lie," her father said, almost as if he had told it. "But imagine learning to post bareback! It must be hard without a saddle and stirrups."

Wendy flashed him a smile and finished her homework. "Don't worry; I'm not going to lie ever again. It's too much *trouble*."

The girls were skipping up the gravel driveway to Holiday Farm the next afternoon when Wendy stopped short. The Masons' old Ford convertible was parked in the yard. "Oh, beans! It's my mother!"

Tim had repeatedly told the girls to get permission to ride. Both their families had agreed, but apparently Wendy's mother had come now to give that permission in person. But if Tim got talking about falls and broken bones, she might think riding too dangerous.

The girls ducked behind the wall to listen. Mrs. Mason was about to get out of the car when the stable door creaked open, and a young voice called, "Good afternoon, ma'am!"

Peeking out, they saw a tall, slender boy of fifteen spring toward the car to open the door. "Did you want to see my father?"

"Yes, please. I'm Mrs. Mason, Wendy's mother."

Wendy and Maureen looked at each other in astonishment. Although the boy was wearing dungarees and a sweater instead of a riding habit, there was no mistaking those blue eyes, those red cheeks, that long neck, and that protruding Adam's apple. And as Tim appeared, there was no doubt whose son the boy was.

After introducing Mrs. Mason to his father, the boy excused himself, saying he had to attend to some errands in Plumbridge. He picked up his bicycle and headed down the drive, waving to the eavesdroppers as he passed.

Mrs. Mason stared after him in a kind of disbelief. "My, goodness! Your son is certainly polite!"

"Brendan? He'd better be! He'd hear from me if he didn't know his manners."

"I stopped by," Mrs. Mason said, "to make sure it was all right, the girls' coming here all the time. I hope they're not getting in your way."

"Oh, I don't mind," he replied airily, "long as they're enjoying it."

Maureen's mouth opened in silent protest. "Enjoying it!" she whispered. "How do you like that! Look at my hands! I can't even get them clean with a scrub brush. So that's what we're doing—enjoying ourselves! Having fun carrying water, tacking up horses, and mucking out stalls, so *he* can sit and read his old *Chronicle!*"

"Shh!" Wendy caught her sleeve as she stood up. "Pipe down or he'll hear you. Anyway, we do have fun . . ."

But Maureen pulled herself free and strode into the yard.

"You've heard of him, Mr. Emmet Phillips, a very wealthy man?" Tim was saying to Mrs. Mason. "He bought one of the ugliest beasts you ever saw. Without my advice. And him knowing nothing about buying horses. What's a man want a . . ."

"Mr. Doyle, you said if we did the stable work, you'd . . ." Maureen's hands were planted on her hips. She wore a determined frown.

"Don't interrupt, girl. Where are your manners?" he said, and went on. "What's a man want a groom for, if not to ask his advice? But no. Not Mr. Phillips. He's dead now, God rest his soul. He simply drives up, and the horse van behind him, and says to me, 'Doyle, I've just bought me a beauty of a horse.' Then they unload him, and I need only one glance. 'You've not bought Beauty, but the Beast,' I tell him. I could see he had everything wrong with him a horse could have— over in the knee, mutton-withered, and I'm supposed to train him and make a show horse out of him! Well, Maureen?"

"We want saddles. You said you'd teach us to ride, and all we've done is jounce around by ourselves!"

Wendy, standing beside her, smiled sheepishly at her mother. "Hi."

"Wait, now; wait a bit," Tim protested. "You'll get lessons and saddles when I think you're ready for them. But it will make more work, remember that. You'll have two saddles to clean. Once you can control your horse bareback, the rest will come easy. Well, jocks, if you're such grand riders, let's see what you can do. And when you're through, there's something I want to show you."

Maureen dashed off to get Little Joe; Wendy hung back. "Mommy, you aren't going to hang around, are you?"

"Oh, no," Mrs. Mason said quickly. "I'm leaving now." She could see that Wendy did not want her to stay. "I'll come watch when you've had a little more practice. Thank you so much, Mr. Doyle, for all you're doing for the girls."

"Not at all. Don't mention it."

When Wendy brought Lady out to the yard and stood on the backless chair to mount, Maureen was already jogging around on the cow pony. "We posted yesterday," she called. "My father says once you're on to it, it's nothing!"

"And that's what you look like—nothing!" Tim commented. "Sit up straight. Get a hollow in your back. Elbows in at your sides. You, too, Wendy. You kids look like a pair of scarecrows. Heels down, for Pete's sake! You look terrible. I'd die of shame if anyone came by and saw you."

Wendy tried to remember all the things Tim said and to post in rhythm with the horse. Up and down, back straight, elbows down—no, that wasn't it—elbows in, *heels* down. Head up, chin in, up and down . . .

The reins cut sharply, and the blister on her left hand broke. The insides of her thighs were sore from having her loose dungarees rub against the pony. Her hands hurt and her muscles ached. Now, as Tim told them they would never make riders, her chin trembled and her nose grew hot. She wanted to jump down and run home, but she went on around until Tim called that it was time to bring the ponies in.

When they had cleaned the bridles and put the ponies in for the night, Tim called them to watch him trim the

horses. He had started with King, using an electric clipper that looked like a giant-sized edition of the kind barbers use.

"Watch this, now, girls, and you'll learn how to clip a horse Irish hunter style."

The big chestnut seemed not to mind as the humming clipper moved over the lower half of his body, shaving the thick hair up to his saddle mark.

"Now he's two-toned, eh, like some of the new automobiles," Tim said, and explained that the purpose of the clipping was to keep the horses from sweating too much in the hunt field. "Hunting's hard on them, too, you know."

He had finished King and was starting to clip Vogue, when a small truck pulled into the yard. "Blazes! There's Fitz. This will have to wait until tomorrow. But don't go, girls. There's more you can learn. Afternoon, Thomas," he called as the blacksmith, a heavy-set man with gray hair and a long, sad face, came into the stable carrying his tools.

The smith answered with a glum nod.

"Nice day," said Tim as the sunshine flooded into the stable.

"Pneumonia weather," said the smith dourly.

"You girls watch Mr. Fitzpatrick, now," Tim said. "He's an artist of the anvil, Fitz is, a man who knows his trade. Yes, girls, a good blacksmith has saved many a life on the hunting field, eh, Tom?"

Thomas Fitzpatrick wordlessly tied on his leather apron and set up his portable forge. The girls watched as he fitted the shoes, heating them in the forge and setting them, hissing, into the water bucket, while Tim told stories of men who had been thrown, yes, and killed, because of a horse that was improperly shod.

All the while the smith said not a word. But when the girls picked up their jackets to leave, he looked up and asked, "Your girls?"

"No, I've just got the one boy. These girls are going to help train the ponies for the boss's kids. *If* they ever learn to ride, that is."

"That boy of yours. He ever ride?" the blacksmith asked.

Tim was silent for so long that the girls thought he had not heard. At last he said, "Not any more. He has a job after school and weekends. Keeps him busy."

"He used to ride, in the shows and all," the smith said.

"Not any more," Tim replied shortly.

CHAPTER FIVE

Santa in the Stable

By Thanksgiving time, when the first skim ice appeared on Acorn Lake, Wendy and Maureen were so used to going daily to the stable that it never occurred to them to stay home. It was second nature, like getting up in the morning. "Or going to school," said Maureen.

Tim was a more demanding instructor, however, than any they had ever had in school. As he had called them to watch while he clipped the horses, and while Fitzpatrick fitted them with new shoes, so he had them stand by when Dr. Cronk, the veterinarian, treated Dan for a swollen tendon and Lady for a cold, and when he himself treated King for a wire cut received hunting. He even had them watch when hay and straw were delivered and signed for, and had them help store it in the stable loft.

They knew enough, by now, to be a real help to Tim. They knew how to mix bran mash and how to pick out hoofs. They were used to tacking up the big horses, standing on an overturned pail to reach up for their heads. If King blew out his stomach when Maureen tried to tighten his girth, she playfully punched him as if he were her brother, and when Vogue refused to open her mouth for the bit, Wendy simply poked her fingers into the mare's gums to make her do so.

The girls were still riding bareback, but riding time was so brief these short days that it did not matter. It was almost dark by the time the stable work was done anyway, without the added work of cleaning the saddles.

By Christmas vacation the ice on Acorn Lake was thick enough for skating. Waking early and seeing the flag her father always put out when the ice was safe, Wendy jumped out of bed. She dressed quickly and ran downstairs with her skates. She and Steven competed every year to be first on the ice; so far he had always won. But his room was directly over hers, and this morning she had not heard a sound from it.

The ice was perfectly clear. By midmorning it would be scribbled all over with marks of skates and sleds. Her own blades would be the first to write upon it! But as she opened the porch door, Wendy saw that someone had beat her to the lake's edge. Not Steven—but Jamie! Well, good for him! Mrs. Mason saw him at the same time and called for him to come in. He had no jacket or cap on, and the temperature was only ten above zero.

"Aw, gee, I'm not cold!" he protested. "I'm sweating!"

"I don't care. Come in and get a jacket."

Grumbling and on the point of tears, he came to the porch as Wendy was lacing her first skate.

"Heck!" he muttered. "And I even ate my breakfast last night, so I could beat Steven on the ice!"

Wendy couldn't help laughing. She took off her skate. "Okay. I'll get your things for you. Then you don't have to take your skates off."

She found Jamie's jacket and cap in the first place she looked —under his bed—and brought them down. Then, just as she had her skates laced, Maureen telephoned. Her mother took the message.

"Maureen says Mr. Doyle wants to see you at the stable right away. He has a surprise for you."

"A surprise? Tell her I'll meet her on the road in two shakes."

She met Steven at the front hall. His racing tubes flashed as he dashed out the door. "Been on the ice? Then haw-haw! I beat you again!"

Wendy smiled complacently. "Yes. But you didn't beat Jamie."

It was bitter cold walking to the stable. The wind stung their eyes, and their breath hung in the air, but the girls were too busy trying to guess Tim's surprise to care.

"Maybe he's got a horse of his own!" Wendy said.

"Baloney! Where would he get the money for a horse?"

"I wonder what it can be, then?"

Tim was in the stable talking with a dark-haired young man whom he introduced as Jerry Owen, the kennelman. He did not stop talking but merely pointed to the saddle rack. There was the girls' surprise! Two saddles, smaller than those used by Tim and Mr. Holiday, had been set there.

"Are those for *us?*" Maureen cried.

"Those are the Holiday children's saddles. You kids can use them on the ponies. That's your Christmas present."

"Hurray! Dibs on Little Joe!" Maureen said quickly.

Both girls admired Lady's appearance, but the cow pony was more spirited, and Maureen always took him when she could.

Wendy led the little mare out of her stall and lifted the saddle onto her back, smoothing the hair under it before tightening the girth.

"Don't get into bad habits now and let your weight rest in the stirrups," Tim warned as the girls mounted. "Knees and thighs, remember. That's where your control is."

Then came the second surprise of the morning. They were

not to be confined to the yard, but were to ride out along the main road with Tim!

Tim, on Vogue, led the way down the gravel drive. Then riding three abreast, they walked the horses eastward to Crane's Corners. Bay, black, and chestnut walked shoulder to shoulder, their breath making frosty plumes in the cold air, their shoes ringing out against the hard surface of the road.

"Aren't we going to trot?" Maureen asked, when at Crane's Corners they turned north.

"Nope. The long up-hill walk is good for their muscles," Tim said. "We'll trot the second half of the square."

Leaving Route 136, they headed west on a dirt road called Lundy's Lane. From here they would go south down Route 42 and eastward again over the main road to the farm. This was what Tim called the square.

At the end of the lane Vogue broke automatically into a trot, and the two ponies followed suit. For a while the girls bounced, as they had done riding bareback, but soon they were able to get into the proper rhythm and to post for long stretches at a time.

"I wish you'd let us have saddles before," Maureen said. "We could have been posting ages ago."

"Learning to ride bareback and to use your leg muscles has given you good riding habits you'd never have gotten if you'd learned in some academy," Tim answered, "where they put you into a saddle the first day and lead you around."

As they approached the farm, the horses, eager to be in, increased their speed, and both girls lost the rhythm once more. But there would be other days, and now they could really post at last.

"Over to one side," Tim said as a car approached and slowed going by. "And touch your cap and say thank you. You'll

be judged by your manners, remember, whether on the road or in the ring."

"What ring?" Maureen asked.

"Why, the show ring. When you're showing the ponies this summer."

That gave them something to think about for the rest of the day.

Cold pricked the insides of their nostrils as the girls walked home late that afternoon, and before they reached Cricket Hill, large snowflakes drifted lazily down to lie at their feet. Maureen tipped her head back to catch a few flakes on her tongue.

"I'll bet it's fun skating in the snow. Is it?"

"Oh, sure."

"Let's meet right after breakfast tomorrow and skate till lunchtime."

"But we promised we'd get over to the stable early," Wendy reminded her. Tim had said that before long they would be helping him exercise the big horses as well as the ponies.

"Okay. When we get back, then."

"Okay." But Wendy knew that the skating would be spoiled by the following afternoon. She remembered from other years how younger children left footprints and marks from sled runners in the snow, and how these froze hard into lumps and ridges. Skating was never as good as before the first snowfall. Then she brightened. She remembered that it was vacation time and that she had no homework.

"Let's go tonight—after supper!"

The girls met at seven, but even by then the snow was fairly thick and impeded their progress across the lake. If it kept on snowing, they would be unable to skate at all until the boys shoveled a rink. And that was usually reserved for ice hockey.

"Oh, well, who cares! We can go sledding."

The snow continued to fall all night, and the following morning the girls walked to Holiday Farm through four inches of it, promising each other that since riding was out of the question, they would return home for their sleds as soon as the stable work was done. But this was a promise they were not to keep.

The yard was empty and the stable strangely quiet as they opened the door. And then they saw Tim lying near Dan's stall, unconscious. For a moment they stood stunned with surprise, wondering what to do. Then Tim moaned and moved his head from side to side.

"Mr. Doyle! What happened? Are you hurt?" Wendy cried.

He put a hand to the floor and tried to push himself up. Then he lay back with a groan. "Get Marge."

"Who?"

Tim did not answer, and Maureen said impatiently, "Never mind, just get somebody. Go see if Brendan's at the cottage. If not, get somebody else."

Wendy ran to the groom's cottage and pounded on the door, but there was no answer. She glanced toward the house where the farmer and his wife lived, but since the red truck was gone from the carriage house, she knew they must be away, for Mr. Metcalf, the farmer, used the truck instead of a car. So Wendy ran to the kennelman's house and banged at his door. The sound of footsteps was reassuring. She sighed thankfully.

Jerry Owen was home, but to Wendy's amazement he came to the door in a bright red suit and black boots, his stomach stuffed out with a pillow. "What's the matter?" he asked.

Wendy was too surprised to speak. As she stood staring, a voice called, "Come on in, whoever it is, and help me get Jerry's beard on!"

A moment later a tall, pleasant-looking woman came to the door, carrying a white beard. "Hi! Are you any good at putting on beards?"

As Wendy continued to stare without speaking, the woman explained. "Jerry's going to be Santa again and deliver the presents at the library. They're having a party in the new Children's Room. This is the third year I've had to put on his beard and make his nose red with my good lipstick!"

"Can you come to the stable?" Wendy managed to say at last. "Mr. Doyle . . ."

The woman dropped the beard and streaked out. Wendy and the kennelman followed. Maureen was kneeling beside the groom when they got there, holding a glass of water. The woman was beside her.

"Tim! Are you all right?"

"Ah, Marge. Yes, I'm all right. Don't worry."

Marge and the kennelman helped Tim to a chair. Maureen's eyes narrowed. "I'll bet I know what it was: Dan kicked him!"

Tim shook his head and put a hand to his eyes. "No, but he backed me against the wall all of a sudden. I fell, and my head must have hit the . . ." He started to get up. "I'll show you."

Marge pushed him down again. "Oh, no you don't! You're going to the doctor's, right now!"

"I'll take him," Jerry Owen said. "My car's right out front."

He returned a few moments later, wearing an overcoat over the red suit, carrying another coat and a blanket. "And here's a pillow," he said, pulling out the one that had been stuffed under his suit.

Tim slumped in the back seat with Marge beside him holding the blanket over him, and Jerry drove off, leaving the girls to take care of the horses. They stayed until the car came back, and Marge and Jerry took Tim into the house. Jerry told them that while Tim was not seriously hurt, the doctor had insisted that he rest for a day or two.

"The horses don't need to go out," the kennelman said, "but maybe you kids can come over and feed and water them. You know more about what they get than I do."

"Sure, we'll come," Maureen promised.

"We'd better not tell anybody what happened," Wendy said as they walked home that afternoon. It had been a frightening thing, seeing Tim—the tallest, strongest, most invincible person they had ever known—lying so still.

Maureen agreed. "They'd think for sure the same thing was going to happen to us. Let's hope he doesn't get talking to my folks at church!"

The girls need not have worried on this score. Far from telling anyone that he had been knocked unconscious, Tim would not admit it—even to himself.

"I must have dozed off, for a minute there," was the most he would say.

"You sure *looked* unconscious," Maureen stated when they were discussing the accident a few days later. "You looked dead to the world."

"*Mau*reen!" Tim always accented the first syllable of her name when he was upset or angry. "What an exaggeration! Can't a man lie down to *rest* himself without people spreading stories?"

"Why, sure." She giggled. "Look at all those people *resting* in the cemetery!"

"As a matter of fact, I was asleep. I remember now, I had a dream. That will prove it! A foolish dream it was, too, for a grown man. I dreamed that Santa Claus came and stood before me, right in the stable."

At this both girls burst out laughing.

"Laugh! I know it sounds ridiculous, but I saw him, all the same. Just as clearly as I see the two of you. And that proves," Tim said with an air of finality, "beyond a doubt that I was sleeping. So let's say no more about it!"

The girls said no more. They could not speak. They were doubled up laughing, and at last, the tears rolling down their cheeks, they slid to the stable floor and lay there overcome with a fit of giggles.

CHAPTER SIX

Banished!

On Christmas morning Wendy found a beautiful pair of white figure-skates beneath the tree, and a blue-and-white skating sweater with matching scarf, mittens, and cap.

"We couldn't decide whether to get you a skating outfit or riding things," Mrs. Mason said, "so we consulted Mr. Doyle."

Tim Doyle had stated firmly that buying new boots or breeches for growing children was a waste of money and that second-hand things would do as well. "You'd only have to be putting them aside and buying them over again in another six months," he said. "So save your money."

The Masons took his advice. Mrs. Mason, who worked part time in an antique shop in Ridgefield, Connecticut, remembered that there was a thrift shop there that displayed riding clothes in its window. And a few weeks after Christmas she and Mrs. O'Mara took the girls over and bought them jodhpurs and boots. From then on riding was easier and more comfortable. The tight jodhpurs were lined with leather to protect their knees, and the boots offered both protection and support.

Unfortunately, the weather gave them little opportunity for riding; January brought deep drifts, and February freezing rain. But regardless of the weather they made their daily trip to the stable, knowing that the horses needed care whether they went out or not. Unable to ride, the girls wandered about the farm, visiting the farmer and his cows or the kennelman and his poodles, or gaping at flowers blooming in the greenhouse as carelessly as if it were June.

At last February, seeming like the longest month of the year rather than the shortest, was over, and on the second day of March Wendy saw the first sign of spring. It was not a robin, nor a crocus, but a flash of bright blue water against the dull gray of the ice at the northern end of Acorn Lake.

"There it is!" Mrs. Mason exclaimed at breakfast. "The first crack in winter's armor!" The wind and open water would work against the ice until it was gone.

In a way, Wendy hated to see the ice break up; her daily visit to the stable had left little time to use her new skates, but on the other hand the end of winter meant more time for riding. Even today, Wendy thought, they might do some real riding, for the hunting season was over and Tim would have more time for them.

Maureen, however, was not on the bus that morning, nor was she on the home-going bus that afternoon. Wondering if her friend was sick, Wendy ran to knock at the O'Maras' back door. Johnny O'Mara came to the door with a spot on his forehead.

"Where's your sister? Is she sick?"

"Have you seen my way gun?" Johnny asked.

"No, I haven't," Wendy answered impatiently. "I don't even know what a *way gun* is, and I asked you a question first."

"It's the one I got for Cwistmas. A wegular way-gun with a wed handle."

Wendy laughed. "Oh. A *ray* gun. If I see it, I'll give it to you. Where's Maureen?"

"Over at the stable. She's been there all day."

"All day!" Wendy echoed. "What about school?" Then Wendy noticed the gray mark on Johnny's forehead and remembered that it was Ash Wednesday. Maureen had told her the parochial children would not have school, but she had forgotten.

She ran home to change her clothes and dashed to the stable. She found it empty. Mr. Metcalf, the farmer, told her that Tim and Maureen had taken the horses to the back field, and pointed the way.

The back field, which marked the end of the Holiday property at Lundy Lane, made a perfect schooling ground, for the land was flat there as it was nowhere else on the rolling acreage of Holiday Farm. A ring of bare earth had been worn through the grass and—less discernible—a figure eight. When she reached the field, Wendy hung back, for two girls in riding habits were mounted on the ponies. She wondered who they were. One of them waved and rode toward her. It was Maureen, in a borrowed hunting cap and jacket.

"Who's that other girl?" Wendy asked.

"Barbara. Barbara Holiday."

"Barbara Holiday!" Wendy exclaimed. "I thought she was a *little* kid! She looks as old as us."

"She's tall for her age. She's only ten. Can't ride for beans, either. Her father wants her to ride, and her mother's afraid she'll get hurt. But guess what I've been doing all day? Jumping. It's lots of fun!"

Wendy put a hand on the cow pony's neck and walked beside it as Maureen rode back to the field, where low jumps only six inches high had been set. That morning, Maureen told her, Tim had put a log on the ground and had her walk Little Joe over it. Then Tim had crossed two logs, and they had gone over them, and had spent the rest of the day taking the low jumps.

"Who are the other people over there?" Wendy hoped she would not have to take her first jumps in front of strangers.

"Just Tim and Brendan. And the lady is Mrs. Holiday. That's why I'm all dressed up. Tim didn't want me riding with precious Barbara in my old dungarees, so they dug up this coat of Brendan's and this old hat of Tim's."

"Maureen! Get over here!" Tim called.

Maureen trotted over. Wendy followed on foot and then stopped to watch from some distance as Tim raised the bar to a foot. "All right? Willing to try it?"

"Sure!" Maureen's shining eyes implied she was willing to jump over the moon if he would let her.

"Good. Steady now. Take him around the ring first."

Maureen clicked her tongue, and Little Joe trotted around the ring and then popped over the bar. Tim turned to Mrs. Holiday. "You see? Not dangerous in the least. This girl never jumped in her life until this afternoon."

"Oh, Mother! Please let me try!" Barbara Holiday was a slender girl, with delicate coloring and her mother's pretty features.

Mrs. Holiday gave a nervous laugh. "Darling, this girl is much older and much sturdier than you. And she's been coming to the stable every day. You're not quite ready to start jumping. And I think you've had enough for today. Get down, now."

"Oh, Mother! Can't I even ride back to the stable?"

Mrs. Holiday eyed the stony path apprehensively.

"Brendan will lead her down," Tim told her. "She'll be safe as a baby in a cradle."

Brendan smiled reassuringly. "Lady's as sure-footed as a goat."

Mrs. Holiday looked after them as he led her daughter and

the pony away, and then got into the car parked on Lundy Lane.

Wendy walked up to Tim. "Is this Barbara's first day on a horse?" She was thinking the girl was pretty plucky; the path back to the stable was rough and in places quite steep.

"First day! Holy saints, she's been riding for two years and not gone beyond a walk and trot. Oh, the girl's willing enough. And you can't exactly blame the mother, either; she saw a man thrown and killed at a polo match and has never forgotten it."

Maureen had taken Little Joe around the ring once more. "I'm going to take the jump again," she called.

"No!" Tim thundered. "Not now. The horse is hot now. You'd better walk him and cool him off."

Maureen, however, put the pony into a fast trot and headed for the jump. At the wings Little Joe suddenly ran out, and Maureen fell. She got up grinning and brushed herself off as Tim ran to catch the pony.

His face was red with anger, and his eyes flashed. Mrs. Holiday's car was just pulling away. "What's the matter with you?" he shouted when it had disappeared down Lundy Lane. "Didn't you hear me? You said you wanted to take that jump, and I said no!"

Maureen hung her head guiltily.

"And look at the pony!" Tim roared. "Sweating! I told you he needed cooling. He'll catch cold, and then we'll have the vet in, and I don't know what all!"

Maureen's cheeks were dark red, and her chin was thrust out angrily. Tim took his handkerchief and rubbed the pony's neck and flanks.

"Fine performance! Falling off in front of the boss's wife, just after I'd told her it was safe! Making a fool and a liar

of me! Well, young lady, you're through! Get out and don't come back!"

Maureen stamped off indignantly. Tim turned upon Wendy, his anger not yet spent.

"And where were you all day, miss? Why weren't you here? You're smaller and younger. I'd hoped to use you for an example, being nearer the girl's age. Having a day off for yourself, eh?"

"Why, I—I was at school," Wendy stammered.

"If you can't be depended on to come when you're needed, you don't have to come at all," he went on.

Wendy felt the sting of tears come to her eyes, and a hard lump in her throat prevented her speaking in her own defense. She wished she had never started riding. Stable work was hard, and Tim was unpredictable. She had been tired, sore, chafed, and blistered since the day they had started. And often she was frightened of Tim.

"I'm disgusted with the pair of you!" Tim muttered as he walked the pony. "I'm through trying to teach you anything! Since you can't be here the one time you're expected, you can just stay home!"

Wendy turned and headed blindly toward the stable.

"Here," Tim called, "take the pony with you; don't be leaving him for me. And don't be leaving your tack for me to clean, either!"

Wendy wanted to remind him that she had used neither saddle nor bridle, and that unlike Maureen and Brendan, she had had school that day, but it was all she could do to keep from crying. She reached out for Little Joe, and he thrust his soft nose toward the pocket where she had often kept an apple for him. This familiar gesture, more than Tim's irate words, brought the tears to her eyes and down her cheeks. But she cried without making a sound, for she was too proud to let Tim hear.

Her heart was heavy as she cleaned the two bridles and the two childrens' saddles, wondering if she would ever get to use them again. Surely Tim ought to realize that what had happened was not her fault. Perhaps she could get up enough courage to tell him.

He was just coming in as she hung the second saddle in the tack room. "Mr. Doyle . . ."

"Well, what is it *now?*" he demanded.

"Nothing. I did everything and I—well, I'm going now."

"Good-by!"

Mrs. Mason's stew was, as usual, rich and flavorful, with lots of meat and vegetables, and few potatoes. But Wendy had no appetite. She sat pushing the food around on her plate.

"What's the matter?" her mother asked.

"Nothing." Wendy slipped a bit of meat onto the paper napkin in her lap.

Under the table Patches' tail went *thump, thump,* and Mr. Mason recognizing the sound, said, "Don't feed the dog at the table."

"I don't care for any dessert," Wendy said a moment later. "May I be excused to do my homework?"

Patches followed her upstairs. In her own room Wendy lay down and then patted the bed until Patches jumped up beside her—although this was forbidden by her mother, who had to wash the bedspread. She put her head down on the dog's furry back and automatically pulled burrs from his neck. So they had been banned from the stable! Well, that was that. There were plenty of other ways they could spend their time!

Doing what, she asked herself. What *could* they do—she and Maureen? What was there to do—in March? Skating was over, and it would be months before they could swim. The ice on the lake was almost all gone, but you could not even go out in a boat for another month, because "they" said the water was too cold. There were still white ribbons of snow left in the shade of stone walls bordering the fields, but you could not sled or ski on them! If you couldn't ride, there was simply nothing in the world to do! *Unfair,* she thought.

A voice from somewhere inside her head told her she *should* be doing homework, and she rose with a sigh to sit at her desk. She opened her history book, but though she read the words, her mind was filled instead with the words that had been said in the back field, and finally those on the page swam together, and she rubbed her eyes with the ends of her pigtails.

No matter which book she opened, she found her thoughts straying back to the groom and to the empty days stretching ahead. It was impossible to study. She decided to get up early and do her homework then, and setting the alarm for six, she put her clock under the pillow so its ring would not wake the family.

I'll never get to sleep, she thought. The clock's steady *tick-it, tick-it* sounded very loud. It seemed to be beating its way into her head—and before she knew it, she had been asleep ten hours, and the alarm was going off.

Morning already? She silenced the alarm and jumped up as she always did to see what kind of day it would be. But it was still dark outside, and gradually the scenes of the day before came back, like a nightmare remembered, but true, and she knew it did not matter what kind of day it was. She would have all afternoon to do nothing but homework. Why bother to get up at all?

She got back into bed and slept until the telephone rang at seven.

"Hi! It's me," Maureen said cheerfully. "I just wanted to tell you to bring your jodhpurs to school. If we leave our things at the stable and get off the bus there, it will save us a half hour."

"But, Maureen! Have you forgotten? He told us not to come back."

Maureen laughed. "That was yesterday afternoon. Last night he called my father and talked for an hour about the show, and he said . . ."

"Show? What show?"

"The P.H.A. The first horse show every year is put on by the Professional Horsemen's Association. Guys like Tim. A friend of his, Bert Buchanan, is running it this year, and Tim wants us to show the ponies."

"Are you sure? I thought he was mad at us."

"That's what he called up for last night. It was his idea that we would have more time if we got off the bus at Holiday Farm. That way, he said, we could get there 'good and airlie,' " she added, imitating Tim's accent.

CHAPTER SEVEN

Wendy Finds a Friend

Tim was studying the program from the P.H.A show of the year before. "Let's see. Lead Line. We'll get Teddy boy into that one on the cow pony and pray to heaven he doesn't tumble off, as he did last year. Old Barbara goes into Walk and Trot again. Maybe she'll get a ribbon this time, poor child. And now we've got to pick a couple of classes for you two jocks."

While the girls went on with the stable work, Tim pored over the program, marking it here and there and speaking more to himself than to them. "Working Hunter—King; Handy Hunter—Vogue. They'll give her a blue unless they're blind or crooked. Heavy Hunter . . ."

The girls grinned at each other. Yesterday was a bad dream. Tim Doyle was as kindly and forgiving as a grandmother—until Maureen led Little Joe into the yard and started to mount.

"Oh, no you don't!" Tim jumped up, overturning his chair, "No, ma'am! You're not riding Little Joe. Not ever again. Lady is your horse. Wendy, from now on, stay off Lady and stick with Little Joe. When it comes to the show—*when* and *if* you should be ready for it—we'll see. Till then, no changing about."

"Why?" Maureen demanded. The mare was a shade too gentle and ladylike for her taste. "You mean I can't ever ride Little Joe again? Just because of yesterday? Why? What did I do wrong?"

Wendy closed her eyes and sighed. Why remind him, she thought. Please, Maureen, she begged silently, don't get him angry again.

"What did you do wrong? Everything!" Yesterday's anger flashed into his eyes and then faded. "But it's not what you did, but what you are," he said quietly. "And that you can't help."

"What do you mean? What am I? What can't I help?"

Tim led Dan into the yard and swung into the saddle. Wendy took the cow pony and handed the mare to Maureen.

"You're too much alike, you and Little Joe," Tim said. "And therefore no good to each other. High-spirited, high-strung, highly nervous, the pair of you." He started out of the yard.

Maureen put her foot into the stirrup and swung her leg over the saddle. "I am not 'nairvus'!"

Tim jogged Dan down the driveway. "You are. Hot-blooded, hotheaded, and hot-tempered. Irish, in other words."

"Ha! Look who's talking!" Maureen clicked to Lady, and they followed Tim out of the yard. Little Joe pricked up his ears, and without urging from Wendy trotted to catch up.

"Just as Wendy and Lady are too much alike," the groom went on as the three walked their horses toward the path. "Placid and easy-going. Lady can do with a bit of fire on her back, and Little Joe needs to be kept calm. So stick to your horses, kids, and we'll be all right."

Tim cantered ahead, leaving the girls to trot up the path beside the groom's cottage, past the old carriage house and along the stony path, which they took single file.

At the top of the hill Wendy looked down to the field and saw that Tim was setting up the bars. Her heart gave a frightened leap. Would Tim remember that she had not jumped at all the day before? Little Joe stopped as if sensing her own wish, but she clicked him on. Might as well get it over with.

The jump was only a foot high, and Maureen took it as if she had been jumping for months. Wendy's heart beat loudly, and her stomach felt cold, as Tim motioned her to take her turn.

"Shouldn't I try walking over a log first?"

"You've nothing to worry about. The horse does the jumping. He's done it many a time before. Just hang on, get your weight forward. Put your hands on his crest."

As Wendy hesitated, Maureen came around at a brisk trot and took the jump again. Little Joe's ears went up, and as Lady went by, he followed.

"Hang on!" Tim called as the cow pony approached the wings. "Eyes straight ahead. Look between his ears. Don't look down, now."

Wendy's heart was beating fast as they approached the fence. Then the pony was taking off, he was up over it and down again, and it was over. She sighed with relief. Then immediately she thought, "I want to do it again! It's fun!"

"So far, so good," said Tim, and he raised the bar six inches higher. "Ready, Wendy?"

"I—I guess so."

"What do you mean, you *guess* so? Brendan's taken that pony over three-foot fences. There's nothing to it."

Maybe for *you*, Wendy thought as she trotted around the track. Her hands were shaking, and her stomach felt hollow. She was not afraid of falling and being hurt, but of looking foolish in front of Tim and Maureen.

She and Little Joe followed Maureen and Lady around the ring, the ponies starting at a trot and going into a canter.

"Okay," Tim called. "Give him plenty of rein, grab his

mane if you want to. Get up out of the saddle when he takes off. Eyes forward. Hold your position!"

Wendy leaned forward, clinging tight with her thighs and calves, and rose up and forward as the pony took off. They were in the air. She felt a moment's exhilaration, and then they were landing. She sank gratefully into the saddle, able to breathe again.

"Well, that was easy enough," Tim commented. "Let's put them up a bit."

Jumping was fun, but Wendy wished Tim would let her get used to the foot-and-a-half jump before raising the bars. "That was fun, but, Mr. Doyle . . ." she began.

"Fun when you've got a good horse," he interrupted, putting the bar up to two feet. "It's when you're on a divil like Dan that you've got something to worry about."

Wendy was relieved when Tim left the fences at two feet and allowed the girls to school the ponies over them all afternoon, taking time between jumps to canter around the field. Tim had been right, Wendy realized, in insisting that they learn to ride without saddles, for now their muscles were trained so that they were secure enough to try almost anything.

From then on, the girls jumped every day and practiced taking the ponies around the figure eight and getting them on their right leads. One Saturday Mr. Mason drove over with his Polaroid camera to take pictures. Wendy told her father just where to stand so as to get Little Joe in mid-air as they took the jump, but Tim, coming into the field at this moment, let out a roar.

"No, no! If there's to be a photographic record, let it be of a horse who's a bit more photogenic. Down, girl, and get up on Lady."

Wendy dismounted, got into the mare's saddle, took her

around the ring, and headed for the jump. Lady, used to Maureen's somewhat greater weight, sailed over the fence with so much room to spare that it might have been set at three-foot-six, and she still would not have touched it. The picture was ready almost by the time Wendy had come round to them, and when her father pulled it from the back of the camera, her heart swelled with pride.

Is that *me*, she thought? Why, I look like a steeplechase rider! There was Lady, her forelegs high, looking like some great prancing statue, and Wendy, her pigtails flying, looking surprisingly small. Her father was smiling proudly, but Tim shook his head sadly over the picture.

"Wendy, Wendy, whatever happened to you? The pony's form is perfect. See how neatly she's tucked up her forelegs? But you . . .! Haven't I always told you to look forward?"

Wendy took another look at the photograph. Her heels were down, her knees tight, her hands in proper position, but she *was* looking down, just a little, to the spot where Lady would land. Wendy sighed. She would never, never ride or jump well enough to please Tim!

The first weeks of April brought such heavy rains that schooling of the ponies had to be abandoned. It rained so steadily that they could not even take the ponies out on the road but exercised them briefly in the yard, bareback. Then, on a Sunday in the middle of the month, the sun shone mistily on a wet world. The drenched grass glistened, Acorn Lake was high, and nearby streams overflowed their banks, leaving puddles everywhere.

The girls danced toward the stable, free at last of raincoats and hats and even of school—for it was Easter vacation. Tim gave them permission to go to the back field alone, but warned them not to go faster than a trot.

"Cantering will cut up the ground too much, now it's so soft from the rain. And no jumping—it's dangerous on a slippery field. A slip in the mud could mean a bad spill for you and a broken leg for the pony. And you know what a broken leg means—a bullet!"

The ground steamed, stone walls sparkled, and evergreens gave free showers as the girls rode to the field. Giggling, her black curls drenched, Maureen rode beneath low branches and shook leftover raindrops down upon Wendy and herself.

"Hey, let's have a race!"

"We'd better not. Tim said not to go beyond a trot," Wendy reminded her.

"Oh, all right." But a moment later Maureen had another idea. "Let's go exploring!"

They took the ponies through a gap in the stone wall into the next field and through the woods. At one point they caught sight of a flashing white tail, as a startled deer took off across their path. At another three fawns stood alert and still until they had passed, and then went leaping away. At last it was lunchtime.

"What a slow, poky ride we've had all morning," Maureen said as they returned to the schooling field. "It's drier now; let's take a few jumps."

"But it's still muddy—the ponies might slip."

"Rats! I just hate this slow stuff. And Lady is soft from all that rest. It would do her good to *go* a little. Come on, let's canter back."

"But he said . . ."

"Chicken?" Maureen challenged. "I don't care—I want to *canter*."

The ponies had been trained to obey the words "trot" and "canter," and Lady immediately went flying down the path

in the direction of the stable. Little Joe's ears went forward
with interest, and he, too, went into a canter, following Lady
with every intention of catching up and overtaking her.

Wendy pulled at the reins. "Trot!" she commanded, and
she called out to Maureen to stop, but her voice was lost under the noisy clatter of hoofs as Little Joe, heedless of the
pressure of the reins, went charging ahead, as if he and the
mare were racing in the Grand National.

Down toward the stable they went, small stones flying out
beneath the ponies' hoofs, past the old carriage house toward
the groom's cottage. There it was that Little Joe's heart's de-
sire was accomplished. He overtook Lady and then, suddenly faced with strange reflections in a puddle, he swerved,
and Wendy was thrown over his head. She landed unhurt in
the puddle and rose, covered with mud, to find the groom
holding the pony and glaring down at her.

"What the devil do you mean, tearing down the path like
that?" he thundered. "Can't you obey? Are you deaf or
just plain dumb?"

Wendy rubbed the mud from her eyes. Mud covered her
jodhpurs and her sweater. Maureen had dismounted and
stood quietly by, holding Lady.

"Didn't I tell you not to canter?" Tim bellowed, outraged.

Wendy was silent, waiting for Maureen to speak. She did
not want to be a tattletale, and how could she explain what
had happened without being one?

"Well, can't you answer even? Did I or didn't I?"

"You did," Wendy whispered.

"Are you crazy, then?" he roared. "Do you want to break
your neck? It's lucky you're not killed. And that the pony's
not got a broken leg. If the boss saw you, he'd have my scalp
for letting you come at all. Well, say something. Don't stand
there like an idiot."

"I'm sorry." Wendy gulped.

"*You're sorry!*" he snorted. "*I'm* sorry to see you can't be trusted to follow simple instructions. Look at you—all covered with mud! Can I send you home like that? What would your parents think of me? Well, get along. Don't just stand around catching pneumonia. Get up to the house and get your wet things off." He pointed toward his own cottage.

Wendy stumbled blindly toward the stone steps, his words following her. "Can't use her head! No more sense than a backward three-year-old moron!"

Wendy wondered how she was to change her clothes, when she had none to change into; during vacation they came to the stable dressed for riding. She wondered, too, if she would be banished from the stable. And she wondered most of all why Maureen had not spoken up.

"Well, if you don't look like a drowned rat!"

Wendy looked up. The smiling woman holding the door open for her was the woman she had seen only once before— the day Tim had seen Santa in the stable.

"Hi. Remember me? I'm Marge Doyle. Come on in." As Wendy stood looking at her with frank surprise, Mrs. Doyle smiled, and a long dimple appeared down each side of her mouth. "Don't you remember—I was helping Jerry with his Santa Claus beard?"

Wendy shook her head. She remembered how concerned Marge had been when Tim was hurt, but she had never supposed that Tim would have a wife like this—so pleasant and smiling and calm. Meanwhile Marge Doyle's dimples had spread into a wide grin.

"I'm sorry," she said, trying not to laugh, "but you do look like a hobgoblin. How'd you like a nice hot bath?"

Marge Doyle helped Wendy off with her sweater and put

it on the porch to dry. "Tell you what: while you're taking your bath, I'll fix us a pot of tea. Okay?"

After Tim's outburst this casual kindness was almost more than Wendy could bear. She ran into the bathroom and closed the door.

"You can use that big towel on the door," Marge called in. "Try not to get everything muddy, will you?"

Ten minutes later Wendy came out, wrapped in the towel and feeling a lot better. Mrs. Doyle had set out an odd collection of clothing for her and was laughing at the sight. Underwear of her own, a shirt and dungarees of Brendan's, and a sweater of Tim's—all very much too large. She left Wendy to put them on and went into the kitchen.

When Wendy was dressed, she looked at herself in the mirror and had to laugh. "Anything for Halloween?" she asked, standing in the doorway.

"You look beautiful! " Marge exclaimed, grinning. "Tea's ready."

A teapot, two cups, and a plate of bread and butter were set on a low table in front of the living-room couch. Wendy sat down. Usually shy with strangers, she felt completely at home with Marge Doyle, as if she were an older sister.

"I'm glad for a chance to talk with one of the wonderful 'jocks' I've been hearing about," Marge said as she poured the tea. "One of Tim's prize jockeys."

Wendy's mouth fell open. "Us? Wonderful? Us? Maureen and me?"

"That's all I've heard. Wendy and Maureen, Maureen and Wendy, all year! Tim was telling me just last night that you kids are two of the best little riders he's ever seen. It's amazing what you've learned in such a short time. Tim says you've both got a good seat and good hands and will make wonderful horsewomen."

Wendy simply could not believe her ears. "Tim—I mean, Mr. Doyle—said that? He always tells us we're practically hopeless."

Marge waved this away with a laugh. "Don't pay any attention to that. He never gives anybody any praise. Thinks it spoils kids. Take Brendan. He was a darned good rider, but his father is such a perfectionist, he finally quit."

Wendy followed Mrs. Doyle's glance toward a framed photograph. It showed Brendan at about twelve years of age, taking a four-foot fence. "They had too many rows; it just wasn't fun any more," she added.

There was no rancor in Mrs. Doyle's voice as she made these remarks. Instead, a matter-of-fact acceptance of the man's nature, as if she were merely saying that he was six-foot-three and too tall for low-ceilinged rooms.

They sat quietly a moment. Wendy's eyes went around the room. It was small, but comfortably furnished with three easy chairs besides the couch, a television set, and a bookcase filled with trophies and books about horses. Copies of *The Chronicle* and *The Blood Horse* and other magazines lay upon the side tables, and pictures of horses—a hunting scene, a photograph, and an oil painting—hung upon the walls. Wendy liked the room; it gave her the same feeling of warmth and ease and friendliness as did the woman sitting beside her.

"How come I've never seen you except that once?" Wendy asked.

"I've got a job in the office of the North Salem school. When Brendan started working after school and weekends, I was so lonesome I just had to do something. Tim's busy with the horses all day, and Brendan doesn't get home until supper-time."

The door opened and Tim's face appeared. "The kid all

right? No bones broken? That's a blessing," he growled, and withdrew his head.

"Know why he yelled at you before?" Marge asked.

Wendy refrained from saying that Tim often yelled at them, taking up her tea and bread instead. It tasted better than Thanksgiving dinner.

"Because he was scared. He thinks a lot of you two kids. He was afraid you might be hurt. Understand?"

Wendy remembered a time, years before, when her brother Jamie had narrowly missed being hit by a car when crossing the street, and how violent their mother's scolding had been.

Marge held the teapot over Wendy's cup, and Wendy nodded for more just to prolong the feeling of cosiness and companionship she felt.

Marge studied her a moment. Suddenly she asked, "Why didn't you tell Tim it was really Maureen's fault?"

For the second time Wendy's mouth fell open.

"I was watching out of the window," Mrs. Doyle said. "But I'd have guessed, anyway. I know the two ponies. Lady has to be urged. Little Joe won't let anyone get ahead of him. I'm surprised Tim didn't guess."

All at once Wendy was glad that Tim had not guessed. When he got angry at Maureen, he got very angry; he might tell her not to come back—and mean it—and riding alone was no fun. "You're not going to tell him, are you?"

"Not if you don't want me to," Marge said.

Several days passed before Maureen mentioned the incident. One evening she came to the Masons' and knocked on Wendy's door. Wendy was at her desk, cutting an item from the local paper.

"I guess you think I'm an awful rat to chicken out like that and let you take the blame the other day," Maureen said in a low voice. "I should have told Tim I started it. I *was* going to tell him the next day," Maureen went on, "but I didn't get a chance. And then the longer I waited, the harder it was. Well, I guess I'd better tell him tomorrow. Only he'll probably be twice as sore and ask me why I took so long to own up. But I'll do it." She started out of the room.

"Wait, Maureen," Wendy called. "It's all over. Let's just skip it." It was wiser, she thought, to let the matter drop. Tim was not angry with her, he had not banished her from the stable, and she had found a good friend in Marge.

"Okay," Maureen said after a moment, but her face was still flushed with embarassment as she murmured, "Anyway, I'm sorry . . ."

"That's all right." Wendy, too, was embarrassed. She changed the subject. "Hey, did you see the announcement in the paper? About the show?"

CHAPTER EIGHT

Heels Down!

"Heels down, a hollow in your back, chin in. Don't push ahead, take your place in line quietly, and look pleasant, as if you were having your picture taken."

The whole month of May Tim had drilled the girls, not only on riding form but on manners in the show ring. The Professional Horsemen's Show was on Memorial Day, and the girls were entered in two classes each.

"No sour looks when you're dismissed," Tim went on. "There's nothing worse than a poor loser. And if your pony's had a good round, and people applaud, remember it's the horse deserves the credit; give it to him with a pat and a few kind words of praise."

Late in the spring they had started schooling the ponies over jumps three feet high, but Tim did not consider their form good enough for competition and he had entered them, therefore, in hack and equitation classes only. This, he said, was mainly for experience.

A few days before the show they hacked up to the show grounds to become familiar with the layout, and while Tim schooled King and Vogue over the fences, the girls practiced in the ring.

The evening before the show the girls went to the stable after supper to help get the horses ready. King and Vogue and the two ponies were groomed until their coats gleamed like satin. Their hoofs were oiled, and saddles and bridles and ironwork were given an extra polish.

"Watch this now, girls," Tim said when his friend Bert Buchanan came to braid the horses' tails. "There's an art to it."

"My mother could braid tails, I bet," Wendy boasted. "She's had plenty of practice on me."

"It's not quite so simple as braiding pigtails." Tim laughed. "But bring her over next time. Maybe she can learn to do the braiding for us and save the boss some money. My heart bleeds for him, poor man," he added with a wink at his friend.

The tails had been washed and brushed. Bert Buchanan stood back of Vogue, grasped her tail, wet it thoroughly with a brush, and began braiding. But though the girls watched closely, they could not see how he did it, so quick and dexterous were his hands. And the result was a neat but complicated braid, ending in a little loop.

As each tail was done, it was wrapped in bandages to protect the braids overnight, and then the braiding of the manes began. The girls could help with this, braiding small strands, looping each little braid back upon itself, and sewing it with strong black thread.

Brendan, meanwhile, was assembling sponges, dandy brush, rubber scrapers, and hoof picks. Bert nodded a greeting. "You going to work for us again this year, Brendan?"

"Sure thing." The boy grinned. "Wouldn't miss it." He would work as jump boy, moving in the wings when needed, and lowering and raising the bars.

"The horses look good, Tim," Bert commented when his work was done.

Tim pulled at his chin. "Now if only per-form-ance comes

up to ap-pear-ance, we'll be all right. Well, jocks, run home now and get your beauty sleep. You've got your outfits ready, have you?"

Their second-hand jodhpurs had been cleaned and their boots polished. Wendy had received a new hunting cap for an Easter present, and Maureen would wear Tim's second-best stuffed with paper. Marge had promised to lend them two of Brendan's old riding jackets. Maureen had worn one of them before, and it fit quite well. It was a winter jacket of black wool, but the velvet collar set off her fair skin and dark hair. The other jacket, of light-weight tweed in the same size, was much too large for Wendy, but with the sleeves turned up it would do.

"You're going to swim, and I'm going to roast," Maureen said with a laugh as they walked home carrying the jackets. "Well, see you in the morning. Don't forget to bring me one of Steve's shirts—and a tie."

"See you at 5 A.M.," Wendy said as they parted on the road at ten.

She was still half asleep when she met Maureen the next morning, but the cool air soon woke them and sent them running at top speed, excited and eager for their first show.

Tim and Brendan were already in the stable, packing up the things they had got ready the night before. The girls, wearing old jeans and sneakers, mucked out the stalls, fed and watered the horses, picked out their hoofs, washed noses and docks, and checked manes and tails for straw.

The sun was just breaking through the morning mist as they finished their work and went to the cottage for breakfast. It would be a sunny day, Tim predicted, but not too warm. A perfect day for the show. Good weather had put Tim in a good mood. "It's fine experience the ponies will be getting this day. And fine experience for you two green jocks as well," he said over his toast and tea.

"Don't forget," Marge reminded the girls, "if either of you gets a ribbon in the hack class, trot right over and hand it to . . ."

"Ribbons!" Tim interrupted. "There's no need worrying them about ribbons, two green riders in their first show. But you're right; in a hack class, girls, they're judging the ponies. And since the ponies belong to the Holiday kids, they get any ribbons that are given. But what judge with eyes in his head would be giving a ribbon to Little Joe? Poor devil, with his big head and short neck."

Marge cleared away the plates. "You kids better get dressed."

Tim hung on to his cup and pointed a finger to hold them in their places. "No, the judge is more likely to laugh at him than give him a prize, but if he does laugh . . ."

"Come on, Dad." Brendan pushed back his chair. "It's getting late."

Tim went on as if no one had spoken. ". . . if he laughs he's just showing his ignorance, for the Lord made Little Joe as he is. He didn't choose to be a cow pony instead of a sleek race-horse at the Calumet Stables."

Marge took the girls into the bedroom to help them get dressed, and Tim was left alone at the table talking about judges. There were not many honest judges left, he was sorry to say, and horse shows were not what they once had been.

When the girls were dressed, Marge tied their ties and then tucked Maureen's curls into a hairnet. Mrs. Mason had done Wendy's pigtails early that morning, but after the stable work they had to be redone. Marge rebraided them, holding Wendy between her knees as she sat on the couch.

"You ought to wear bandages on them—like the other ponies," Brendan said with a smile, and Wendy threw a sofa pillow at him.

"Brendan! Bren-dan!" Tim bellowed from the bedroom. "What about my boots?"

Brendan had gone to pack the lunch into the farm station wagon in which he and his mother would ride to the show. Tim came out in his best breeches and brown socks. "My boots haven't been shined!"

Since the girls were ready, they got to work polishing Tim's best boots. Marge was washing up the breakfast dishes.

"Marge! Where are you?" Tim called. "Tie my stock, will you?"

At last they were all ready. The van was parked at the road, and Tim led the horses down the driveway and up the ramp. When Vogue and King were loaded, Brendan brought out the ponies. Lady allowed herself to be led into the waiting van, but Little Joe planted his hoofs firmly at the edge of the ramp and would not budge.

"Bound to get one poor loader out of four," the driver commented.

"Not us," Tim boasted. "All our horses are good loaders. He's just waiting for his girl friend. Hop up, Wendy, and lead him up."

Wendy ducked under the rail, and Little Joe clambered up after her. Then Maureen ran up the ramp, and the door was closed with girls and horses inside. Tim sat beside the driver.

"You all right back there?" he called as the van started down the road.

Maureen answered with a whinny, and Wendy gave another. They rode sitting on the floor, hands and noses cold with excitement, enjoying the dark interior with its familiar odor, like a stable on wheels.

Half an hour later the driver swung into the show grounds to park beside the other vans. The door slid back and sunlight flooded the van. The girls jumped up and led the horses out. The whole place was bustling with activity. Horses were being schooled and walked. Vans were pulling up, grooms were busy giving horses and tack a last-minute polish while children in smart habits rushed to the judges' tent.

Marge and Brendan came hurrying toward the van. They had parked the station wagon at the ringside, near the cars of the O'Maras and the Masons. They helped remove bandages from the horses' tails. A mane braid had come undone. "Holy hat! We forgot the sewing kit!" Tim cried.

But no, Marge had remembered it, and the braid was re-done. Now the girls were sent for programs and numbers. When they returned, Marge hooked the round placards to their jackets, and Tim went over the program with them. Class No. 6 was first.

"Why not Class 1?" Maureen demanded.

"Why doesn't money grow on gooseberry bushes? Don't ask me! No. 6 is the Lead Line. Teddy and Little Joe, Lord help them both."

The little Holiday boy, in jodhpurs, a tweed jacket and brown velvet hunting cap, was brought to them by his sister. Barbara, looking slender and pretty in her blue-and-gray tweed coat, smiled shyly at the girls.

"Good luck, both of you."

"Thanks. Same to you."

Marge fastened Teddy's number to his back, and Tim lifted him onto the saddle. "There you go. Hold the pony's head, Barbara."

And now a voice, made tinny by the amplifier, came over the loudspeaker: *Ladies and gentlemen. Your attention, please. Entries for Class No. 6, be ready at the in-gate.*

"There you go, Teddy boy. No tears, now. You're a big boy," Marge said.

Barbara led him off, and Tim said, "He'll be a big man like his father."

The girls followed to watch. Their parents called to them. They merely waved. Older brothers and sisters led younger ones into the ring on sleek ponies and fat ponies and shaggy Shetlands.

"*Aah!*" came from the crowd. "How cute!"

They circled the ring a few times, and lined up. The judges were smiling. There were ribbons enough for all entries, and the children left happily holding up the fluttering colors.

"I got a blue!" six-year-old Teddy crowed, holding up the pink ribbon he had been given.

"Sure you did! Good for you!" Marge said admiringly, lifting him down.

Little Joe was brought back to the van. Maureen's class was next.

Entries for Children's Hack, Class No. 17, ready at the gate, please.

"Good luck, Maureen!"

"Hollow in your back. Heels down. Smile."

Maureen and Lady waited their turn at the in-gate. They were next-to-last in the ring. Lady went through the walk, trot, and canter, as if horse shows were an everyday affair to her. *Reverse, please.* The riders turned and walked, trotted, and cantered in the opposite direction. Then they lined up while the judges compared notes, and Maureen was among those dismissed.

"Never mind, you did as well as any of them," Marge assured her.

"Lady went like an angel!" Wendy cried, and Tim said

soothingly, "Can't expect a ribbon your first time in the ring. What's coming up?"

The girls could not watch the next class, for the horses had to be walked between classes, but when Class No. 22 was announced, they put the ponies in the van and raced to watch Tim ride King in the Working Hunter division.

The fences were set at four feet, but King sailed over them as easily as if he had wings, and won the ribbon and the prize money. The girls hugged each other gleefully and ran to congratulate the chestnut gelding as he came out, blue ribbon at his cheek.

"Better get Lady out here and see that Barbara is ready," said Tim.

Barbara Holiday entered the Walk and Trot and was awarded a yellow. "That's great!" Wendy said, as she took the pony after the class. "Next year you'll have to enter Walk, Trot, and Canter."

Next came Class No. 26, Wendy on Little Joe in Children's Equitation. Little Joe took orders well and went through the class without hesitation or error, and Wendy smiled with pride. "I don't care what Tim says," she murmured to him as the riders lined up and he backed neatly into place. "You're a beautiful little pony. There's not one that's a bit better. Your first show, and you didn't do a thing wrong!"

Now the names of the winners were announced over the loudspeaker, and the ribbons handed up. *First, Miss Susan Channing. . . . Second, Miss JoAnn Noyes. . . . Third, Master Woodley Babcock . . .* on through six ribbons, and then, unbelievably, Wendy heard her own name: *. . . and Reserve, Miss Wendy Mason.*

Her cheeks flushed with pleasure, and she patted Little Joe lovingly. "See? What did I tell you? You're as good as any of them."

The winners of the blue and red and yellow ribbons were applauded as they rode out, then the other three, and Wendy alone was left. She sat waiting on her pony, but nothing happened. Even the steward was walking away toward the judges' stand, leaving her all alone in the ring.

She heard Tim calling to her from the rail. "It's over. What are you waiting for?"

Tim must have missed the announcement, she thought. Surely she had not just imagined that they had called her name! She would have much preferred trotting out to sitting alone there, all eyes upon her, but if Little Joe had won a ribbon, she wanted him to have it.

And then the steward, a short, bandy-legged fellow in red coat and white breeches, came back. "There's no ribbon given for Reserve, Miss." He spoke in a kindly way, but Wendy's cheeks flamed.

"What happened? Did you fall asleep out there?" Tim asked, and told her that six ribbons were all that were ever given. "Blue, red, yellow, white, green, pink. If only they gave a lavender, now, you'd have been okay," he told her with a sympathetic grin.

After the luncheon recess the girls entered another class each, but were not in the ribbons, and then, their ponies through for the day, they were free to watch the afternoon events. They had only to inspect Vogue and hold her in readiness for Tim to take on the outside course.

This class was like a steeplechase, with a high brush jump, a post-and-rail, a stone wall, and, after a sharp turn, five more fences. They climbed upon the fence to watch. The horses took the course one at a time, and when at last Tim appeared at the starting point, they heard people all about them exclaim, "Beautiful animal! . . . Just look at that mare! . . . Isn't she a beauty!"

The girls almost burst with pride. Vogue's coat gleamed in the afternoon sun. Her muscles rippled. And then she was thundering over the course like a black giantess, coming to the jumps at a gallop and taking each in perfect form. The wait for the announcement was filled with almost unbearable suspense. But at last it came. *First, Latest Vogue, owned by Mr. and Mrs. Carter Holiday of Holiday Farm.*

Tim invited the girls to dinner with his family, but by the time they reached the restaurant, the girls were too tired to eat. They had got to bed late the night before, had risen early, and rushed about the entire day. The show over, they had ridden back in the van, helped unload the horses, watered and fed them, and cleaned the tack. They ordered hamburgers, but were too sleepy to eat them, and sat heavy-eyed and yawning as the Doyles discussed the day's events.

"Well, kids," Marge said, "you didn't win any ribbons, but you did every bit as well as those kids riding their own horses, didn't they, Tim?"

"They're far from perfect," he said. "They've a lot to learn."

Marge was hot in their defense. "What do you mean, weren't perfect! What did they do wrong? Nothing! And they'd been up since dawn. The girls they were competing with didn't have a thing to do but get themselves ready and have grooms give them their horses. These two . . ."

"All right, Marge. I'm not saying they didn't do fairly well for a pair of green jocks," Tim admitted. "They might even be in the ribbons someday."

CHAPTER NINE
In the Ribbons

On the morning of the Hunt Club Show in mid-June, the door of the horse van closed on a gray sky, and by the time the driver turned into the show grounds, the girls heard the splatter of drops upon the roof.

"Looks like rain on and off all day," Tim said. "But we might as well get started."

In a heavy shower, everything was done as before—horses were led out and tails unbandaged and inspected, the girls ran for programs and numbers and returned soaked. They walked the horses to loosen them up and rode through their first classes with rain beating into their faces.

"Smile!" Tim called, as Maureen entered Children's Equitation. "You're not riding to your doom!"

Maureen smiled, had a good round, and won a red ribbon. Dismounting, she gave the ribbon to her mother and the mare to Wendy, who was riding her in the next hack class.

"What a beautiful little mare!" Wendy heard someone remark as she waited at the in-gate. Her heart swelled proudly. Sometimes she felt she loved Lady best of all the Holiday horses, she was so well mannered and so dependable, and every point of her conformation perfect. It was no surprise to her, therefore, when Lady won another ribbon—this time a yellow.

Leaving the ring, Wendy patted the mare to tell her that the applause and ribbon were for her, and then trotted over to where the Holidays' car was parked and reached in the window to give the ribbon—her very first—to Barbara.

"Well done. Congratulations," said Mr. Holiday.

"Thank you." Wendy turned the horse, but heard the horn tooted behind her. Barbara Holiday was holding out the ribbon.

"You keep it, Wendy."

"Oh, no. They were judging the horse, not the rider."

"Please. I want you to," Barbara insisted with a smile, so Wendy accepted it and trotted happily over to her parents, who pinned it to the visor of the car.

It alternately rained and drizzled all morning. Spectators sat in their cars, the windows tight, watching through streaming windshields, while the scheduled classes went on just as if the sun were shining.

"Typical horse-show weather!" Wendy heard from grooms and owners on every side, as she and Maureen readied the horses for their classes. Mrs. Mason had brought a short plastic rain-cape with a hood for Wendy, but it got in her way, and Wendy was afraid its rustle might make Little Joe nervous, so she took it off.

This time, in their various classes, Wendy and Maureen recognized several girls with whom they had competed in the earlier show. Now, sitting mounted and waiting on Lady and Little Joe, they saw the Channing sisters of Roundabout Farm and JoAnn Noyes of Bright Brook and Laura Forbes, whose father was master of foxhounds. These girls recognized them, too, and smiled and nodded and chatted about the show, while rain dripped from the brims of their velvet hunting caps, drenched their well-tailored jackets, and made dark blotches on their made-to-order jodhpurs.

"I wish Diane Channing would be careful of those jodhpurs," Maureen said, as she and Wendy went to the Masons' car at luncheon recess. "I may be wearing them next year!"

Wendy let out a shout of laughter. "Hey, I wonder if Laura Forbes recognized these I'm wearing. They still have her name tape in them!"

"Say, wouldn't it be awful if they wanted their things back?" Maureen asked, as they got into the car and Mrs. Mason handed them each a chicken leg. "They're certainly good sports, though, sitting there in the rain just like anybody else."

Mr. Mason smiled at the girls in the rear-view mirror and paraphrased a verse of Robert Louis Stevenson's:

> "The rain is raining down in pools,
>   It rains on ships at sea,
>   And on the girls from private schools,
>   The same as you and me."

The girls howled with pleasure and got him to repeat it, and when they had finished eating and the sun came out faintly, strode around the show grounds repeating it over and over.

The day of the Horse and Pony Show, two weeks later, the July sun shone brightly, and Tim predicted a good day for the Holiday horses. The girls did better this time, Maureen winning a yellow and Wendy a green on Lady, and Wendy a red and Maureen a yellow with Little Joe. At noon they compared lunches. "Swap you half a ham sandwich for a deviled egg." "Give you some potato chips for a couple of pickles."

After exchanging several items, they walked to the refreshment truck to buy soft drinks. A gray-haired man in a riding habit turned to smile at them. "Afternoon. Good to see the sun again."

They nodded, recognizing him immediately. But apparently Colonel Kirby did not see any resemblance between these girls in riding clothes and the dungaree-clad pair who had visited his riding academy.

"You're Carter Holiday's girls, aren't you?"

"No, we just ride his horses," Maureen answered.

"You've been doing pretty well for yourselves, ribbons in every class you've entered. How'd you like to show a pony for me?"

The girls were silent. They did not want to ride any pony of his and were not sure Tim would allow it.

"I've got a nice little pony I'd like to enter in the hack class," he said, "but the girl who used to show him is in Europe this summer."

Wendy said, "I don't think Mr. Doyle would . . ."

"Tim Doyle? Why, I've known him for years! Let's go see what he says."

Taking them by the shoulders, he steered them to the ring, where Tim was talking with Bert Buchanan.

"Oh, Dan's not so bad," Tim was saying. "He's got his faults, but I've cured horses of bad habits before."

"Then how about starting on some of your own?" Bert said with a grin.

Tim laughed heartily and turned to the Colonel. "Afternoon, Colonel. What can I do for you?"

Colonel Kirby explained that he hoped one of the girls would be allowed to show one of his ponies in the next class.

"It's okay with me. How do they feel about it?"

They looked at him pleadingly, the words "Do we have to?" written plainly upon their faces.

"They're a bit tired," Tim said. "Up since dawn, getting the old ponies ready. But you know, girls," he said, giving them a meaningful look, "the Colonel here is a friend of Mr. Holiday's, and any friend of his ought to be a friend of yours—right?"

Sighing, the girls agreed reluctantly and left with the Colonel to look at his pony. It was a picture-book Shetland with a round nose and a tail that touched the ground.

"Isn't he a pretty little fellow?" the Colonel asked, straightening the red ribbons braided into the mane. "Name's Lollipop."

As the girls stood beside the pony, it was obvious that Maureen was so tall that she would look ridiculous upon his back. "But you'd be just right," the Colonel told Wendy, and hurried off to enter the pony and get a new number for Wendy.

"Lollipop!" she scoffed, kicking at the grass with her heel. "A nice entry for the lead-line class!"

Mounted, she felt enormous. Compared to this pony, Little Joe was a full-sized horse! But Lollipop responded well to her hands and legs, and as she took him to the lower field for a practice ride, she had to admit he was well trained. The field was set with jumps for a later event, and to Wendy's surprise the little Shetland made straight for the first fence.

"Oh, no you don't!" She turned him aside. "What do you think you are—a big steeplechase horse?" She liked him in spite of herself.

The Colonel was waiting at the in-gate with her number, and hooked it over the one she was wearing. Wendy blushed with embarrassment; it was a large class, and all the riders were younger than herself. She could only hope that among so many she would be unnoticed as they all went into the ring and went around at a walk, a trot, and then at a canter. *Reverse, please.* Lollipop had a nice way of going, responding to the slightest pressure of her knees.

"Good boy! You're a little peach!" she said, patting the pony with affection, and then felt annoyed with herself for being so disloyal to the Holiday horses.

A great many of the riders had been excused by now, and

Wendy was among six kept in the ring. But she was too pleased with the little pony's way of going to mind being the largest in the group. Standing in line, waiting for the announcement, Wendy was surprised to see Brendan and another jump boy carrying out the wings and setting up bars between them. She looked around at Tim, who stood at the rail.

"It's all right," he said. "They're low. Go ahead. It says, 'Best six may be required to jump.'"

The six jumped in turn. The bars were set at only a foot and a half, and Lollipop sailed over them with ease, winning the blue. Wendy felt slightly embarrassed when the ribbon was handed to her, for the other riders were only eight and nine and ten, but it was nice winning a blue all the same, and she smiled happily as she pinned it to the pony's band.

"Congratulations, Lollipop," said Colonel Kirby. "And thank you," he added to Wendy, taking the pony as she dismounted. "Perhaps you can ride him for me again next year."

"Next year she'll be even bigger," Maureen pointed out just as Tim walked up.

"Well, Wendy, how did you make out?" he asked, as if he had not been right there at the rail, watching.

"She got a blue," said Maureen.

"No!" Tim looked incredulous, putting on a kind of false innocence. "Where is it, then?"

Wendy glanced toward the Colonel, who had just taken the blue ribbon from the pony's headband and put it in his pocket.

"Well, well! So you got a blue," said Tim. "Your very first!" He gave the Colonel a smile. "Would you believe these two girls had not had much more than three months' riding experience?" he asked conversationally. "There's no riding to speak of in winter, you know, and these kids had never been on a horse until they came to see me last October. They'd tried

to rent horses at one of these fancy, high-priced stables—I don't know where it was—and the owner wanted to charge them an arm and a leg for lessons. And them mere children dying to ride. Ah, well, takes all kinds to make a world, does it not, Colonel?"

"That's right. See you around, Tim." The Colonel moved off with his pony.

Tim shook his head, scowling. "Never mind, Wendy, you'll be taking other blues, and it's not likely he'll ever get another, poor man, with those goose-rumped, ewe-necked, slab-sided, sway-backed mules he's got."

The girls walked back to the van, laughing over Tim's words. A cooling sheet had been hung on a line strung between two trees. Back of it a groom was schooling a white horse over a jump. The horse refused.

"Gedd up, there!" the man snarled, and slashed at the horse's head with his crop. The girls stood in horror.

"Hey!" Maureen shouted. "You can't do that!"

The groom glared at her. "Mind your business, girl."

Wendy pulled her away, and they saw that the name on the van was Boots and Bridles. Wendy shivered. Was that why Lollipop was such an obedient little pony? Had he been beaten into submission?

"I'm going to save my money and buy that pony!" she declared. But the next moment she knew she would never have enough. And she had no place to keep a pony. And he was much too small for her.

At their own van she rubbed her nose against Little Joe's cheek. "I'd like to see anybody treat *you* like that!"

"Little Joe's your favorite, isn't he?" Maureen asked, biting into an apple and giving the rest of it to Lady.

"Of our horses, you mean? No, I like them all."

"But suppose you could have one for your very own. Which one would you take? Know who I'd take? Dan."

"I wouldn't take any," Wendy said honestly. She liked Little Joe because he was 'her' pony. But certainly Lady was nicer in lots of ways. And King Donegal was undoubtedly the best all-around horse in the stable. And Vogue was the most beautiful animal in the world. And Dan—well, he was a devil, but naturally she liked him, too.

"Wouldn't you take one for your own if you could have him?" the other girl persisted.

Wendy shook her head. "Why should I take *one?* This way I've got *five*." She had what she had always considered ideal—a whole stableful of horses!

CHAPTER TEN

In Charge of the Stable

The horse shows went on all through the summer, and one day late in August, Tim called the girls into the cottage for a serious talk. His vacation was coming, and rather than hire a man, as he had done in other years, he preferred leaving them in charge.

"You know the horses. You know the routine. They're used to you. But it's a great responsibility. Think you can do it?"

"Yes!" Both girls answered at once.

Tim nodded. "I think you can. And if you should need help or advice, Jerry will be here, and the old man. And the vet's number is in the tack room."

"Sure they can do it," Marge said, smiling at the girls.

Tim cocked an eye at Maureen. "What about our Wild Irish Rose, here? I hope she won't be up to any of her tricks—trying to jump over the milkhouse or anything."

"She'll behave," Marge assured him. "At least—while we're away," she added, winking at Maureen.

"All right then, you're in charge, you two. I'm putting a lot of faith in you. And the boss is putting his faith in me—that my judgment of you is sound."

So the three Doyles left for the seashore, and Wendy and Maureen became head grooms. Their routine, actually, was little different than before, for to ease the work, Tim had suggested they leave the ponies in the field, making two less stalls to clean. They arrived early in the morning, exercised the big horses, looked them over afterward, groomed them, cleaned tack, mucked out, spread clean straw, fed, and watered. In the afternoon they walked to the field and rode the ponies bareback to save the bother of cleaning their saddles, and when neither working nor riding, they fooled around the farm, playing with Teapot—the Metcalfs' cat—chasing the ornamental fowl kept by the farmer's wife, or visiting Jerry and the poodles.

After five days a postcard came from Marge: "Tim and Brendan having wonderful rest. How are the horses?"

The horses were fine, except that Vogue had a few sores on the heel of her left hind leg. They asked Mr. Metcalf, the farmer, to look at it.

"Do you think we ought to call the vet?"

"Cronk? Not him!" The old man shook his head. "He don't like animals, Cronk. I think he's afraid of horses."

But when the sores increased and Jerry shook his head over them, they called the veterinarian. He examined the big mare thoroughly, but in such a gingerly manner that the girls wondered if what the farmer had said about him was not true.

"Is it bad?" Maureen asked.

"Not too bad," Dr. Cronk replied. "She's got mud fever. I'll give you a blister to put on it. Rub it in three or four times a day. She'll be all right."

He gave the salve to Wendy, and she rubbed it in as soon as he was gone. That evening she and Maureen returned to rub in a second application. They walked home slowly. It had been a warm day, and the evening brought little relief. The air was heavy, and there was not even enough breeze to lift the willow fronds at the lake's edge.

Wendy went to bed without even a sheet over her. At two-thirty in the morning a crack of thunder split the sky, and the rain came down. She jumped up to close her window. Lightning flashed and a sharp tingle—not a ring—came from the telephone. Wendy suddenly remembered that the ponies were outside. Rain would not hurt them, but they might be frightened by the thunder and lightning.

She pulled dungarees over her pajamas, picked up a denim jacket that Steven had outgrown, and ran outside to tap at Maureen's window. Maureen's face appeared immediately. "Think we ought to go over?"

"Yes," Wendy said. "Put something over your pajamas, and bring a flashlight."

Maureen came out with a scarf over her head and a sweater over her shoulders—but no flashlight. "We had one, but Johnny took it apart."

"I know." Wendy sighed. "That's what happens to all of ours. We keep getting them, but we never have one. That's boys for you."

The road was pitch-black. They stumbled along through the darkness, hurrying down the road without speaking. Their shoes went *squnch, squnch* at every step, and they were wet to the skin by the time they reached the main road. Being together, it seemed fun. Being out in a downpour in the middle of the night was an adventure, and the wetter they got, the harder they laughed.

Their feet slid over the stones on the steep path to the field, and once Wendy slipped and scratched her arm. They were glad they had come, though, when Little Joe's whinny greeted them, and Lady stepped out from under a tree as if waiting for her escort to take her home. The mare and the cow pony had been sheltering under a thickly leafed maple and were not nearly so wet as their rescuers.

In the stable the girls rubbed the ponies down and put them in their stalls. Then they looked at themselves and burst out laughing. Water was running from their hair in rivulets and dripping from their clothes. Maureen wrung out her sweater and scarf.

"Maybe there's something here we can change into."

Wendy's teeth had begun to chatter. She took off her shoes and poured the water out, but the stone floor was cold. A red flannel shirt of Tim's hung near the stable door, and the tack room yielded a suede vest of Mr. Holiday's. In the barn a ragged sweater was found in a corner.

"Probably Teapot had her last litter of kittens on it," Maureen said.

But these things were better than nothing. The girls took off their clothes, dried themselves with cooling sheets, and curled up in horse blankets. Old Mr. Metcalf found them at five in the morning.

"Wake up and go home! You've no business sleeping here!"

"We were worried about the ponies."

"They're all right. You girls get on home. Mr. Doyle is coming back today. He'll take care of everything."

"Today! But they've only been gone a week and a half."

"We got a postal card. They want to miss the Labor Day traffic. Don't blame them. More cars on the road every year. 'S awful!" The old man shuffled off, shaking a finger at them. "Go on, now. Get home."

When they unwrapped the blankets and looked at themselves, they decided to take his advice. It would be awful if anyone saw them dressed as they were, and their own clothes were soaking wet. The flannel shirt came to Wendy's knees. The sleeves hung over her finger tips. "How do I look?"

Maureen, in the ragged sweater and suede vest, minced around with one hand on her hip. "How about me? Do you think I should wear this to the Ritz tonight?"

"Absolutely! It's simply the latest vogue."

Hearing her name, the black mare nickered softly, and the girls stared at each other, ashamed that they had forgotten her. They raced to Vogue's stall, and Maureen picked up her hoof. "It's worse!" she cried. "That blister only made it worse! That dopey Cronk! What does he know? A man who's afraid of horses!"

Wendy took the can of salve and sniffed it uncertainly. "Should I put it on or not? He said . . ."

"No! Throw it away!"

Wendy hesitated. The hoof did look inflamed, but did they

dare leave it untreated? Perhaps without the salve the mud fever might have developed into something worse. The blister had a sharp, medicinal odor. She wished there were some way to test it.

She thought of the cut on her arm. The blister ought not to sting any worse than iodine. She rubbed some on. It stung, but unlike iodine, it kept on stinging. The girls left the stable, and by the time they reached the lake, Wendy's whole arm was throbbing. Washing with soap and water helped only while the cool water was on the scrape. She put on clean pajamas, tiptoed into her parents' room, and took a jar from her mother's dressing table. The face cream was cool and soothing, and almost as soon as her head touched the pillow, she was asleep.

"Nothing to worry about," Dr. Cronk assured Maureen when she telephoned him from Jerry Owen's house later that morning. "That's what a blister's for. Works like a counter-irritant. It's bound to look worse before it gets better."

"Should we keep putting it on?"

"Of course."

"He says to keep putting it on," Maureen told Wendy. "But *I* wouldn't. I'd chuck it out."

Wendy, however, had decided upon a compromise. She went in to take care of the mare, while Maureen got the saddles from the tack room and started tacking up King and Dan. A few minutes later the girls led the chestnut and roan into the yard and then hacked up to Crane's Corners and back. Returning, they rode the ponies to the back field, left them there, and walked back to finish the stable work. When they had picked up the five stalls, Wendy paid another visit to Vogue and then joined Maureen outside, where they sat upon the stone wall to await the Doyles.

Their eyes heavy with lack of sleep, they took turns lying down upon the wall and going down the driveway to look up the road. And of everyone who came in or went out of the farm—Jerry, the mailman, the farmer and Mrs. Metcalf— they asked the time. The morning seemed two days long!

At last a horn sounded. The green Plymouth came chugging up the driveway, and the girls shouted, "They're home! They're home!"

Anyone seeing their wild leaps down the driveway, or hearing their shrieks of joy, would have supposed that the girls' families had just returned from the wilds of Africa. Every vestige of sleepiness was gone as the girls dashed toward the car.

"Hey, you're back! Marge! Brendan! Mr. Doyle! You're back!" They threw themselves upon Marge as she tried to get out of the car. Laughing, she hugged them both at once and complained that they were knocking her breath out. Tim rumpled Maureen's hair and tweaked Wendy's pigtails.

"Well, kids?"

"Oh, gosh! It's good to see you. Did you have a good vacation?"

"Sure!" Marge answered. "They had a good time fishing, and I had a *wonderful* time cleaning and cooking fish!"

Brendan held up a soggy package. "That reminds me: I brought you a present."

Maureen held her nose. "Thanks a lot—but no, thanks."

Wendy backed away from it. "So solly. No likee."

Marge had brought them felt beanies and T-shirts decorated with leaping dolphins. Tim presented them with a huge box of candy, which he said was actually from the boss.

"He wanted to pay you, you know, same as a hired man. But I said, 'Nothing doing.' Never accept money, girls, or you'll lose your amateur standing. You've got to keep your amateur standing if you want to ride in the Garden some day. Well, jocks, how did it go? How're the horses?"

In their excitement they had forgotten about Vogue. They

told him the mare had mud fever, and that Dr. Cronk had given them a blister for it.

"Let's see it," he said, striding to the stable.

Maureen handed him the can. "What in blazes!" Tim cried. "This blasted blister is too strong. What you want is something soothing, not an irritant."

He hurried into the mare's stall and picked up her hoof. "Hm, not too bad. I was afraid that stuff might lame her. How often did you put it on?"

Maureen looked at Wendy; applying the blister had been her job.

"I only used that once. After that I—well, it made my arm hurt so much that I—I mixed it with something." Wendy gave him the jar she had brought from home. It was of shell-pink porcelain, with a satin ribbon around the top. Tim read the label, then threw back his head and roared.

"Elizabeth Arden's beauty cream—mixed with Cronk's blister! Well, I'll be darned! But it did the trick!"

He made a tour of inspection then, looking over the horses in turn and admiring the neatness of the stable and tack room. "Well, jocks, everything looks fine. You've a lot to commend you. And now I think you deserve a holiday."

"A holiday? What for?"

"Why, it's Labor Day! I'm sure you'd like spending it at home."

As neither girl showed any enthusiasm for this idea, he added, "At least, I'm sure your parents would like to see something of you for a change."

The girls walked home slowly. For nearly a year the word "holiday" had meant only one thing—a whole day to spend at the stable. What good was a holiday if you had to stay home? But a notice tacked to the bulletin board at Acorn Lake changed their minds.

LABOR DAY SWIMMING EVENTS. FUN FOR ALL.
RACES! PRIZES! EVERYBODY COME!

Wendy dashed into the house to look for her bathing suit, unworn all summer. It was a little tight but free from holes. Grabbing a towel, she ran through the kitchen to the porch and down the sloping lawn to the lake.

Frogs leaped away from the grassy bank at her approach. A turtle sunning himself upon a rock slipped *plop* into the water. Standing on the shore, Wendy caught hold of a willow branch, took a running jump, and dropped into the water. Rising to the surface, she turned upon her back and kicked, sending plumes of sparkling water into the air.

To think she had not been swimming all summer, with the lake right there at her door! She had spent all those hot afternoons on the dusty road, or in the field or at the stable. She went down, down, down as far as she could to where springs made the water cooler. Mmm, it felt good. Suddenly she remembered she had had no breakfast or lunch. A minute later she was back in the kitchen, leaving big, wet footmarks on the red linoleum, her pigtails dripping on her shoulders.

"If you *must* go around in a wet suit," her mother said with a sigh, "at least you don't need to have a wet head!" She began undoing the pigtails.

"Ouch! Let me do it myself!" Wendy pulled off the rubber bands and combed her fingers through her long hair. Then she shook her head at Patches, giving him a shower. "See? How do *you* like it? That's what you do to us when you come in out of the rain."

Patches scratched at the door, and she let him out. Steven came down for lunch as Wendy was eating cereal, her head bent over the bowl, her uncombed hair spread over her shoulders. He held out a hand.

"Here, Patches. Here, Patches." he said, looking toward his sister. "Oh, excuse me," he said when she looked up. "I thought it was the dog."

"Woof!" Wendy snapped her teeth at him. "Going in the races?"

"I might enter the canoe race."

The program began at two o'clock with a tube race for the smallest swimmers, and a prize for each—an ice-cream cone. Next came a race for girls from seven to ten, and after that a balloon race, and then a diving contest for boys. Johnny O'Mara announced that he would do a "Jap knife dive" and put his hands together and flopped into the water. Its sting against his round stomach surprised him, but the applause was gratifying.

Wendy sat on the bench. The sun felt warm. Her suit was almost dry. Her brother Jamie came to sit beside her. The sun touched his close-cropped blond hair, making it look iridescent. The blue of the lake was broken up into a million diamonds, and sapphires sparkled from the paddles as teen-age boys went out in their canoes to the starting place.

Wendy looked around the beach. Small children were playing with pails and toy boats. Babies were eating sand. High-school girls looked like models in their pretty suits. And everyone was tanned *all over*, not just on hands and face as she and Maureen were. How had they got so brown, Wendy wondered.

Why, she realized slowly, for them the entire summer had been like this—a lazy time of doing nothing. A two-month holiday! Imagine doing nothing but sun and swim and sail and play—all summer long! How odd to think that just a year ago she had done the same thing herself.

The next minute the canoes were coming in, and Wendy

was shouting herself hoarse. "Come on, Steven! Oh, come on! Try!"

Steven appeared to be not even trying to win. He paddled casually as if racing were somehow beneath him, but at the last minute he gave a sudden burst of speed, putting all his strength behind the paddle, and while Wendy screamed to him to hurry, he managed to win by inches, when he might have won by lengths.

"Oh, you!" she said as he stepped from the canoe. "You had me worried."

He grinned and shrugged, and accepted the medal awarded with great nonchalance. "No sweat to that."

Then the whistle was blowing for the race for teen-age girls, and Wendy got up.

"Are you sure you want to go in this one, honey?" her mother asked. "The other girls are much older, and you haven't been in the water all summer."

"I don't care. I'm just going in for fun."

At first Wendy was able to keep up with the teen-age girls, but when they started to gain, she decided to swim under water for speed. Unfortunately, she got off course and came in last. Maureen got third prize.

"Hey, I got gypped," Wendy said, coming to sit beside her. "I should have got a booby prize, anyway."

The last event was open to everyone. A greased melon was tossed into the water, and at the sound of the whistle swimmers of all ages dove after it. Wendy managed to get hold of it once, but a big boy put one hand on the melon and the other on her head and pushed her under. By the time she came up, sputtering and coughing, the melon was far away.

For a long while it seemed that no one would ever bring it in. The slippery melon would bob to the surface and then disappear amidst wild splashing. Then it disappeared for good. The boys kept diving and accused each other of foul play. Meanwhile Maureen and Wendy, working as a team, were swimming with it under water, taking turns pushing the melon ahead of them. They sneaked up on the far side of the dock and brought it triumphantly to shore.

Immediately a shout went up, and the boys rushed in, hoping to break the melon open and eat it there on the beach. But Maureen covered it with her towel and gave it to her father for safekeeping.

"We've got other plans for that melon!"

Tim Doyle had expressed a fondness for watermelon. They would carry it to the farm that very evening, put it in the milkhouse to cool, and the next day they would all have a wonderful watermelon party!

And so they might have—except for a frightening accident.

CHAPTER ELEVEN
A Narrow Escape

One moment the stable yard was dreamily quiet, the only sound the drone of bees in the orchard. The next moment the quiet was shattered by a screech of nails against wood, a shout, a crash, and oaths.

Tim had been sitting quietly reading *The Chronicle*. Maureen was perched atop the stone wall. Vogue, her lead fastened to the stable, stood half dozing in the sun. The late afternoon sun gilded Wendy's hair as she groomed the big mare and turned Vogue's black coat to satin.

"Wake up, Lazy, and let me have your hoof," Wendy said.

Tim, his backless chair tipped against the wall, had just found an item of interest. "Now here," he said, speaking more to himself than to the girls, "is an animal worth taking a look at."

"Let's see." Maureen jumped down from the wall in front of Vogue. That was when it happened.

At Maureen's sudden appearance from nowhere, the mare started in fright, reared up, and then jerked forward. Her strap was hooked to a long screw in the wooden window frame, and the sudden jerk pulled out the entire frame, which flew straight toward Wendy.

Before Tim could shout a warning, it had landed in the yard, missing Wendy's head by inches. In an instant Tim was holding the plunging mare.

"Whoa-up. Hold on!"

It took a moment for Tim to realize what had happened, and then he was shouting, red in the face, at Maureen.

"By the saints, what do you think you're doing? Jumping into the yard, right at the horse's head, like a kangaroo! Do you realize that Wendy might have been killed? An inch closer, and she would have been dead. Lying here dead! Killed in a flash, and nothing we could do about it!

"And do you know what else?" he roared. "Vogue might have taken off with the frame banging her from behind, and it could have broken her legs!"

Tim freed Vogue's lead from its hook, and as Wendy led her away, patting her neck and speaking soothingly, he hefted the heavy frame and then shook it at Maureen.

"How'd you like to be hit in the head with this, eh? What an idiot! Does human life mean nothing to you? Haven't you the sense to take simple precautions? No! You haven't learned a thing, for all the time I've spent with you! Christmas! No more sense than one of Metcalf's cows!"

An angry flush mounted to Maureen's cheeks. "You can't yell at me! You're not my father!"

Tim could hardly speak. With a long, shaking finger he pointed to the gate. "Get out," he said hoarsely. "And stay out!"

Marge, Jerry, and the Metcalfs had come to their doors to see what had happened. Maureen strode down the driveway, her cheeks flaming.

"Don't be coming back, now!" Tim shouted after her. "I mean it this time! You stay away from here! For good!"

Jerry Owen walked over to examine the place from which the window frame had been torn. "Hmph! Pulled the nails clean out! And they were big ones, too!"

"Oh, she's strong as an ox, that mare. Lord help us! Did you see what happened? Missed that child's head by an inch! Dead in a flash, she'd have been. And who'd have been responsible?" Tim's voice rose again with anger. "I would! And what would I have said to her parents?"

He turned to Wendy. "You'd better get on up to the house and have Marge give you a bit of something," he said, his voice shaking. "You're all upset, and no wonder."

"Me?" Wendy was still not sure what had happened.

Tim ran a finger around the neck of his shirt collar, and his Adam's apple bobbed nervously. "Yes, you're still shaky, and I don't blame you. Missing your death by a hair." He pointed a trembling finger toward the cottage. "Obey me, now. Go up."

Wendy went as far as the cottage steps. Marge met her there with a glass of milk and a cooky. When she had finished them, she and Marge joined Tim.

"Now, Wendy, you know what you're dealing with when you've got the reins in your hands. Dynamite!" Tim told her. "Man has nothing to pit against such strength but his intelligence."

Wendy got out the stable broom and swept up the broken glass.

"What's the very first thing I told you kids?" he went on. "Never run at a horse. Wasn't that it? A horse will shy at a shadow, or a bird darting, or a leaf trembling, let alone a great girl like that coming down at him. What's the matter with children these days?"

"All right, but don't scold Wendy," Marge said. "She didn't do it." She gave Wendy a smile. "Don't forget: you're staying to supper."

Marge put a wicker table under a big chestnut tree beside the wall, and when Brendan came home from work, Tim told him of the near accident.

"I tell you I thought she was a goner. It didn't miss her by more than a fraction of an inch. It must have grazed you, Wendy. What's that red mark on your arm there?"

Wendy rubbed at her arm. "That's where I scratched myself falling and rubbed Doc Cronk's blister stuff on. It was getting better when Dan nipped me. And I was just taking him his water."

Tim shook his head. "A repository of faults, that animal."

Wendy had a theory about Dan: he must have been mistreated by a former owner.

Tim laughed at this. "Dan was formerly owned by an elderly lady who never drove over twenty miles an hour, as they say in the used-car advertisements. No, Wendy, some horses are just born mean. They're like people, you know. Fitzpatrick, now. Would you ever believe a man like that with the face of doom on him could be related to anyone as jolly as his brother Hugh? Hugh, there in the A & P, with a grin wide as a wagon for every customer. I remember a man back in Ireland . . ."

"Time for watermelon!" Marge put in quickly. "Brendan, run and ask Jerry if he'd like some. Wendy, you come give me a hand."

In the kitchen Wendy eyed the melon pensively. She and Maureen had won it together. "Isn't Maureen going to get any?" she asked.

"Don't worry," Marge answered, cutting the big melon in two with a sharp knife. "I'm sending this half over to the O'Maras'."

Wendy nodded. That was only fair. Still, Maureen would miss all the fun.

Marge covered half the melon with waxed paper and cut the rest into five pieces. "Let's get the dishes out of the way first, shall we? I can never enjoy my dessert when I've got a pile of dirty dishes waiting for me."

The dishes washed and dried, Wendy was sent outside to ask if the men wanted coffee. They were again discussing what had happened in the yard.

"Puts me in mind of something happened when I was working for Mr. Emmet Phillips in Westport," Tim was relating. "I had a horse of my own then, a gelding. Half-bred. Perfect hunter. Great, strong shoulders. I had him tied to a stake, and a fellow working in the stable picked a cooling sheet off the wall and gave it a flick. *Whoom!* That gelding took off like a demon was after him. Pulled the stake out of the ground and ran off with it batting him in the hind legs and . . ."

"Mr. Doyle, Marge wants to know if you want . . ."

"And he fell and broke his leg," Tim went on, "and of course I had to shoot him."

Wendy tried again. "Mr. Doyle, do you and Mr. Owen want . . ."

"And after I shot my horse, I went after that fool who'd flipped that blanket, and punched him in the nose, and after that . . ."

Wendy gave up and went back to the cottage to say she had been unable to interrupt Tim to find out about the coffee.

"Poor Jerry!" Marge said. "He's a captive audience."

"What's that?"

"Why, since Jerry's been invited to have melon, he has to listen. And you know Tim when he gets started! Jerry's caught. Caught like a rabbit in a trap!"

Marge and Wendy carried the melon slices outside and served them picnic style, without plates or forks but with plenty of paper napkins.

For a while they ate without speaking, making slurpy sounds of enjoyment. Then, after a juicy interval, Tim said,

"Yes, I lost the chance to make a lot of money when that gelding had to be put down."

Wendy shuddered. How dreadful it must have been for Tim to have to shoot a horse, especially a fine hunter like that.

"Prize money, you mean?" asked Jerry.

"I do not, man! I mean resale. That's why I bought him. To train him and show him and then to sell him to the highest bidder."

Wendy licked pink juice from her chin. "If he was such a good hunter, I should think you'd have wanted to keep him."

Tim snorted. "I'm not a rich man to keep horses as pets." He leaned back against the tree, keeping the melon balanced in his lap. "To me, a horse is a challenge. Can he take orders properly? Can he learn? Until he can, he's a challenge, and I'm interested. After that, I'm wanting a new challenge."

"Like Dan," Brendan put in.

Tim held a black watermelon seed between his fingers. "If only Dan's brain were this large, we might get somewhere. As it is, we're opponents. He wants to throw me down and break my neck; I want to knock some sense in that thick skull of his."

The next moment, something struck Wendy on the cheek. She turned accusingly. "Mr. Doyle! What was that?"

Tim raised his eyebrows in exaggerated innocence. "What?"

"You know perfectly well something hit me."

"Did it?" Tim held his hand palm upward and looked at the cloudless blue sky.

"A raindrop, most likely. Did you feel a bit of rain, Marge? Look there, Wendy. Isn't the sky darkening in the west?"

She turned, and another seed hit her, this time on the chin. She shot a seed back at the groom. Brendan shot another, and then the battle was on. Seeds showered through the air as everyone joined in the fight. Marge was the first to retreat, and Jerry was next, leaving Wendy to battle both Tim and Brendan.

"Hey! No fair! Two against one!" she cried, and Tim withdrew, leaving the other two to finish it out. Wendy's seeds gone, she broke her rind on a rock and threw the pieces. Brendan was about to do the same, when he had a better idea. Grabbing Wendy by the back of the neck, he rubbed her face in the pink pulp until she gave up. "Uncle!" She pulled away, cheeks rosy and dripping, to fall laughing among the chestnut hulls.

That was the way the summer ended.

School began a day later. It came as a shock. After two months spent in dungarees or jodhpurs and boots, Wendy had to wear dresses or skirts and blouses. Worse, she had only two hours with the horses.

It was lonely walking to the stable without Maureen. The mile and a half from Acorn Lake seemed twice as long as before. Without Maureen to goad her on and set an example by her daring, Wendy wondered if she would have the courage to do all that Tim expected of her. He expected her to help school Vogue, who was sixteen-and-a-half hands high, and King, as if they were ponies. Wendy loved the black mare, but could not help remembering the frightening display of her strength in the yard.

Still, she enjoyed the challenge of riding her, and Vogue behaved well, even when a red sports car came roaring around a curve one day, and Dan, carrying Tim, shied.

On these rides, almost more than at any other time, Wendy missed Maureen and wished she had not been banished from the stable. They had often disagreed, but exercising the horses was no fun without her. Perhaps, Wendy thought, if she had started riding alone, she might enjoy it, but she and Maureen had learned to ride together and for over a year now had ridden together every day. Riding without Maureen simply did not seem natural. She often thought of asking Mr. Doyle if Maureen might not be allowed back, but did not quite dare to do so.

There were rewards, however. Marge telephoned one Friday evening to ask if Wendy would like to drive with her to see the hunt meet. "Be here early tomorrow, no later than six."

The morning air was cool and crisp. The lake was misted with fog. Bluejays shrieked and scolded as Wendy walked to Holiday Farm, and a rabbit scooted across her path. The trees were golden, and poison ivy wound scarlet garlands up tree trunks and along stone walls. The horse van passed her on the main road, and the driver, recognizing her, waved.

"Who've you got in there?" she called.

"His Majesty King Donegal and the big black mare," Halloran replied.

Marge met her at the cottage door. "You're going to see the most beautiful sight you ever saw in your life!" she promised.

Five minutes later the Doyles' old green Plymouth was heading toward Hollyberry Farm, where the first formal meet of the season was being held. Marge was driving. Wendy was beside her. Tim had driven to the meet with Mr. Holiday.

As they reached the estate, Marge slowed the car and pulled into the driveway to park well out of the way, for sleek convertibles, sports cars, and horse vans were arriving every minute. On the broad lawn back of a large white brick house, the master, the two whips, and the huntsman in their red coats were mounted and waiting. Their horses were beautiful—a black, a brown, and two chestnuts. Hounds, alert and impatient, were milling around at the horses' feet. It was an exciting and colorful sight—horses, hounds, and red-coated hunters against the whitewashed brick, and back of it all the flaming hills of the Lewisboro countryside.

"Why, there's Mr. Holiday!" Wendy said in surprise, recognizing him in a red coat and top hat. "Maureen ought to see that!" Wendy exclaimed. "Do you think he'll ever let her come back?"

"I don't know," Marge replied. "You'll have to ask Tim."

The field had gathered. Women in black coats with white stocks and canary vests, others whose black coats were collared in red, men in black coats and red, and others in tweed, sat awaiting the huntsman's signal. He blew his horn, and they all started off.

"It must be fun to go hunting," Wendy said with a sigh.

Marge started to say something, then changed her mind. "May as well stay out of the way," she said instead. The vans and a few cars were blocking the driveway.

"This wheel is cold," Marge said. "See if my gloves are in my purse there, will you?"

As Wendy opened Marge's purse, she noticed the initials M.B.D. in metal letters on one side, and asked what the "B" stood for.

"Bannerman. My maiden name."

"Bannerman! That's not Irish!"

Marge laughed. "Everybody doesn't have to be Irish, you know."

Wendy laughed too. She had often felt that everybody was Irish but herself—Tim, Brendan, the O'Maras, grooms, van drivers, blacksmiths—why, even the horses seemed Irish! And all she had was one grandmother who was Scotch-Irish. She rested her head against the seat, looked at Marge, and sighed.

Marge gave her a side glance. "It *would* be nice to hunt, wouldn't it? Too bad you couldn't go sometime." Her face was serious, but a little twitch appeared at the side of her mouth.

CHAPTER TWELVE

Tally Ho!

"If you hear 'Ware wire,' or 'Ware hole,' pass the word along. And if you hear 'Huntsman, please,' that means to back your horse out of the way and let the huntsman by."

It was two weeks later, and Tim was explaining rules and phrases of hunting to Wendy. She had been invited to join junior members of the hunt club on a midweek meet the next morning at Roundabout Farm, and her mother had telephoned the school principal, asking that she be excused that day.

As Roundabout Farm was only four miles from Holiday Farm, Tim and Wendy hacked to the meet on Vogue and Little Joe. The sun was just touching the treetops as they rode up to the estate. The Holidays' car was already there, and Barbara and her father were getting out. Their horses, Lady and King, had come up in the van.

"Remember," Tim said to Wendy, "you're Barbara's guest, and I'm her groom, and since she can't take the jumps, we've got to stick with her. We'll stay well to the rear with the young kids and go through the gaps."

Wendy had no time to be disappointed. The horn sounded on the morning air, and the master led the way out of the grounds. The field followed, with Barbara Holiday, Wendy, and the other children and their grooms at the rear. They went down a dirt road for a mile or two, crossed a highway,

and turned down a narrow lane. Up ahead the hounds suddenly gave voice and scrambled up a bank. Over the stone wall
they went and into a meadow beyond. The horses followed,
jumping over the wall and galloping off at the other side.
Wendy looked after these riders enviously. Still, this was

better than trying to follow in a car, as she had done several times recently with Marge. Having to stay back with the children must be much worse for Tim than for her, she thought, as they cantered along the road to a gap in the wall.

At the far side of the meadow the hounds tore over another

wall and down a steep incline to the road. Here they went back and forth uncertainly, and those in the rear had time to catch up with the field. All at once the cry "Tallyho!" was heard, and a moment later Wendy caught sight of the red-brown fur of a fox darting through the thick vines at the foot of the wall. The hounds came after him, all speaking at once, but the fox had disappeared. Up and down the bank, up onto the wall and down again, they searched for the quarry. At last they gave up and turned down the road.

For three hours the fox managed to elude them, and then the hunt was over. Even without taking the jumps, it had been a wonderful experience. Wendy could not wait to go again.

"Maybe another time you'll get in a real hunt," Tim said, back at the stable. "At least you saw the fox. It's not often we get so much as a glimpse of him."

Tim seemed in such a good mood that Wendy ventured to ask the question that had been on her lips for so long. "Can Maureen ever come back and ride again?"

Tim's face grew serious. "I don't know about that," he said after a long pause. "I'd have to be very certain that she'd obey orders and show some sense." Tim rubbed thoughtfully at Vogue's saddle. "Perhaps she's not so eager to return as you think. I've seen her many a time at the church, and she's never so much as offered an apology."

Wendy pricked up her ears. If an apology was all that was needed, her days of riding and doing the stable work alone might be over. She would tell Maureen that very afternoon.

"Nevertheless," Tim went on as if reading her thoughts, "she could offer me all the apologies and excuses in the world, and I'd not let her back—not for another month or two, anyway. A promise, that's what it needs," he said. "A firm promise that she'll do nothing to cause accidents again."

Okay, Wendy thought, smiling to herself, an apology and a promise. Tim was weakening. He probably missed Maureen too, for in spite of her quick temper—or perhaps because of it—he was fond of Maureen.

They were still doing the stable work when Marge came back from her work in the school office. "Well, Wendy, how was it? Have fun?" she asked, her eyes brimming with pleasure. "Gosh, I'm glad you got to go! Isn't Roundabout Farm magnificent? Who was there?"

Wendy's tongue went to the corner of her mouth as she tried to remember. "Let's see. Swampfire and Gentleman Jim and Soundwave, and that new liver-chestnut of Regan's, Chianti . . ."

Marge brought her purse down on Wendy's head. "You! I meant what people! Not what horses! You'd make a fine society reporter! Send you to a ball at the Plaza, and you'd come back and tell us about the hackmen's horses outside!"

One day early in December, when Wendy and Tim had just returned from riding, Maureen came to the stable. She opened the door just wide enough to see Tim at the sink inside.

"Mr. Doyle? May I come in?"

Tim looked up. "Eh? What for?"

"I—I just wanted to talk to you."

"Well, talk is cheap. Come in, then. It's drafty. We'll all be catching cold."

Wendy was in the first stall, filling Vogue's pail. Tim busied himself at the saddle rack for a few moments. "Well, speak up."

"I wanted to say—I'm awful sorry for what I did, frightening Vogue that way. I know it was a dumb thing to do. I wouldn't ever do anything like that again. So . . . do you think I could come back?"

Tim considered this a while. "It's a great responsibility,

having kids around a stable," he began, and gave Maureen a long talking-to. But Wendy knew from his face and from the tone of his voice that he was going to say yes. She flashed a grin at Maureen, but Maureen was looking steadily at Tim.

"Let's see," Tim said, having concluded his lecture. "How long has it been now? Two months? Three? Do you think you can control your temper? Can you remember my instructions?"

"I know I can remember your instructions. About my temper . . ." She grinned uncertainly. "I'll try."

He looked at her affectionately. "Good enough! You can come back, then. We might even arrange for you to go on a hunt."

Maureen's eyes danced. "That would be neat!"

"Of course, on your first hunt, you'll have to stay back with Barbara and go through the gaps instead of taking the jumps. Your father not being a millionaire member of the Hunt Club, Mr. Holiday will be paying your capping fee. So you'll stick with his daughter."

"No jumps! What fun is it without jumping? Gee, I don't want to stay in the back and play nursemaid to . . ." Maureen suddenly broke off, swallowed, and said quietly, "Okay. That would be fine."

"That's more like it," Tim said approvingly. "I'll see what I can do."

The girls were walking to the cottage to say hello to Marge, when Brendan came home from his job.

"Well, well, look who's back! I guess I know why she came back—she missed her boy friend Dan. Was that it, Maureen?"

"Sure! He looks just like you—only his ears are shorter!"

Brendan picked up the hull of a horse chestnut and threw it. Maureen threw one back, and the next minute he was chasing her with a handful of dried hulls, through the vegetable garden and around the kennels, until she popped into the greenhouse for safety.

The following week Maureen went hunting, and after Christmas, when Barbara Holiday went to Bermuda with her mother, both Wendy and Maureen were invited again to hunt. This time they took stone walls and rail fences with the rest of the field, were in on the kill, and came home in triumph.

During January each girl went hunting again, and then it was February, and the hunting season was over.

The snow that fell the first Saturday in February was surprisingly light. It all but blew away when Steven Mason, clearing the driveway, tossed a shovelful over his sister's head as she came outside.

"Hey! Look out for Spooky!" Wendy cried.

Mr. Metcalf had given each of the girls a kitten from Teapot's latest litter. Wendy's was coal-black. He lifted a paw and shook it free of snow, only to put it down again and step into feathery crystals up to his nose. Spooky shook his head and backed into a snowdrift. Wendy caught him up and set him in a cleared spot and waded across the road to the O'Maras'.

Maureen came out pulling on her mittens. "If this keeps up, Fitzpatrick will have to take the Neverslips off the horses and put on real snowshoes!"

It was one of those winter days, rare in February, when the sky is blue as in June. Wendy threw handfuls of snow joyfully in the air. As they walked along, they knocked snow from evergreens onto their own and each other's heads. It touched their cheeks like cold flower petals and clung to their lashes in sparkling drops. At a rise in the road they looked down at the lake. It was dotted with skaters and dogs and marked with the black lines of skate blades.

"I love to skate in the snow," Wendy said, "especially when it's light like this and your skates go right through it."

She had gone skating on Christmas Day and could almost make a figure eight. "Let's see if we can get through early and have some time to skate before supper."

"Or else we could put on the lights at the clubhouse to-night," Maureen suggested.

The lawn in front of the farmer's cottage was a tempting expanse of pure white.

"Let's make angels!"

Wendy lay down on her back and moved her arms in a wide arc. Maureen was helping her up when they heard hoofbeats. Looking around, they were surprised to see King coming down the driveway, his tack hanging loose. Maureen ran over and caught him. "How the heck did you get out?"

As they led him back to the yard, they saw Tim coming from behind the greenhouse with Dan.

"Know what this blasted idiot did just now? Jumped right over the yard wall! Would you believe it! Won't jump when I want him to, but takes it into his head to jump a five-foot wall!"

Shortly afterward, when the snowplow had cleared the road, they took the horses out, Maureen riding King, Wendy on Vogue, and Tim lecturing Dan as if he were human.

"Just you wait, Mister Captain Dan! Wait until spring! Then your schooling will start, and you'll find your school-master is not one to be easy with you. You'll have long hours and no recess nor holidays. And, Danny boy, you'll jump as *I* want you to jump!"

In spite of the blue sky the day was bitterly cold, and the girls were glad to get back to the stable after two hours, and then into the cottage where Marge's tea, strong as coffee and cooled with milk, awaited them. Over tea, Tim told his wife about Dan's escapade.

"How high is that wall? Six feet, would you say?"

"No, but *you* would." Marge laughed, for Tim had a habit of exaggerating.

"Seriously," said Tim, "we've never had a horse jump that wall since we've been here. And how long is that? Let's see, I was thirty-five when we came, and I'll be forty-one this month. That means . . ."

"This month? What day?" the girls wanted to know.

"The twenty-seventh. But I don't have birthdays any more." Tim drained his cup. "I'm too old for that nonsense."

Nevertheless, the girls immediately began making plans for a birthday surprise. They would take as many baby-sitting jobs as they could and buy him a wonderful present.

That evening they called to invite Brendan to come skating. Accompanied by Steven, they met him at the clubhouse. The sky was velvety and starless, but lights twinkled in the houses all around. There were no sounds, either, but those of their own voices and the *shhh shhh* of their blades through the light snow.

When the girls were tired, they sat upon the dock, talking, while Steven and Brendan shoveled a rink and then raced around it and spread-eagled and tried other stunts. After a while Brendan skated toward them and did a rink stop, showering the girls with ice shavings.

"What are you two plotting here?"

"We're trying to think what to give your father for his birthday."

"I'm giving him a wool shirt if I can afford it." Brendan skated away and came back. "Hey, I know something he needs. A wallet. His old one's a mess."

The girls were delighted with the suggestion. February, however, proved a poor month for baby sitters. Ice storms, high drifts, and frozen ruts made driving so difficult that residents of Acorn Lake went out only when absolutely necessary. The result was that neither Wendy nor Maureen earned any money all month. Their earlier savings had gone with Christmas, and they had nothing but their allowances.

"Four dollars," Maureen said mournfully. "Well, I guess we can get some kind of wallet for four dollars."

"Three ninety-five," Wendy said realistically. "That'll leave five cents for a card."

One snowy day Mr. O'Mara put chains on his tires and drove them to Mount Kisco, where there were several men's shops. After an hour of looking and comparing prices, the girls chose a wallet of tan cowhide, decided upon more by price than appearance, and then spent another half-hour selecting a card.

"Here's a good one for him." Maureen giggled. "It says: 'I used to be conceited, but I got over that . . . and now I'm perfect.'"

Tim had a sense of humor, but Wendy was afraid he might be offended. She thought it safer to send an ordinary birthday card. Besides, she pointed out, they could not afford a humorous card; they cost twenty-five cents.

On Tim's birthday Marge invited the girls to stay to supper and cooked a pheasant Brendan had shot in Putnam County in the fall. The cook had kept it in the freezer at the big house for them. It tasted just like chicken—only better, the girls assured Marge.

And then, while the tea was brewing, Tim picked up his packages. Wendy pulled her chair closer, and Maureen grinned and wiggled impatiently. Tim opened a large, flat package and took out a red flannel shirt. It was from Brendan.

"Well, now, isn't that fine! Real wool, is it? No, it couldn't be! Yes, by thunder, 100 per cent wool, it says on the label. That ought to keep the old bones warm."

Next he picked up the small package from the girls. Maureen bit her lips, and Wendy held her breath. Tim admired the ribbon, the paper, and the card. "*From your two jocks.* Now what can that be?"

"Open it and find out," Marge urged, seeing the girls' impatience.

"I'll open it in time. I'm just taking proper notice of the entire package. Who did this up—you, Wendy?"

"No, the man at the store."

"He did, eh? Well, think of that! Such fancy work! I'd have said it was done by a woman's hand, wouldn't you, Marge?"

"Oh, for Pete's sake—open it!"

"It's so pretty I hate to spoil the wrapping," he said. "Maybe I'll let it sit there a bit."

He put it down and opened the gift from Marge—a beautiful wallet of fine pigskin, with gold metal at the corners, two bill compartments, and six transparent envelopes for cards. While Tim exclaimed over the quality of the leather, and the convenience of its many compartments, the girls looked stricken. Wendy stared staight ahead, her eyes wide and ready to fill with tears of disappointment.

At last Tim opened their gift. There was an embarrassed silence. Then he said, "Well, what do you know! *Another* wallet! You must have been ashamed of me, all three, carrying that shabby old one! Isn't this fine?"

Marge reached for it. "What a nice, sturdy one. This cowhide wears like iron."

"You can take it back and get something else," Maureen told him, her cheeks red.

"Take it back! I'll do nothing of the kind!"

"But you've got that nice one from Marge," Wendy said miserably. "You don't want two."

"Don't I, though! Two is just what I do want! One for every day and one for Sundays. Yours is good-looking, Marge, but it's a bit dainty for regular use."

"Ours hasn't got all those nice compartments," Maureen pursued.

Tim opened the pigskin wallet and flipped through them. "What are they for, anyway?" he asked as Marge went to get the cake. "Tens, twenties, fifties? Who has money like that?"

"The envelopes are for cards," Brendan told him.

"Cards? Then there are not enough. Ace, King, Queen, Jack, ten, nine. That's all."

"*Identification* cards."

"Identification! If any man wants to know my identity, let him ask me, and I'll tell him!" Tim rubbed his hands together with satisfaction. "Well, well, a nice red flannel shirt and two wallets! I feel like a rich man. Has Mr. Holiday got two, I wonder?"

The girls sighed contentedly. Marge put the cake before him, and Tim blew out all the candles with one breath.

"What did you wish for?" Wendy asked, as they put on their rubber boots to go home.

Tim closed one eye. "Ah, but that's telling. And told wishes never come true."

CHAPTER THIRTEEN

The Stray Horse

The weather was still far from springlike when, on St. Patrick's Day, early in the morning, Marge telephoned to ask if Wendy would like to drive into the city to see the St. Patrick's Day parade.

"Maureen's coming. Shall we pick you up, too?"

But St. Patrick's Day was not a legal holiday at the Lewisboro public school, and Mrs. Mason refused to write an excuse. Wendy had been excused several times during the hunting season, and her mother saw no reason for her missing another day of school just to see a parade.

"You wouldn't like it anyway—standing in the cold trying to see over people's heads," Mrs. Mason said as she braided Wendy's hair. And Mr. Mason maintained that St. Patrick's was the one day he wished he could stay home. He hated crowds, the traffic was terrible, and it was worth your life to cross Fifth Avenue to the library.

Wendy was not reconciled. She was annoyed with her parents and angry with the whole world. She liked parades, even if her parents did not. She did not mind crowds, nor standing in the cold. If they thought *that* was bad, she said to herself rebelliously, how would they like riding in freezing temperatures with the wind smarting their eyes and numbing their hands on the reins!

She sulked through her classes, thinking how unfair it was

that the parochial-school children should get all these saints' days off, and the regular holidays as well. *Unfair*, she thought as she got on the afternoon bus. And *unfair*, she was still thinking as she scuffed up the driveway at Holiday Farm. What fun was it to ride alone? None!

As she stamped across the stable yard, she pictured the Doyles and Maureen having fun in New York, and kicked the cottage steps. Marge had left the key under the mat so Wendy could get in and change into her riding clothes. Wendy was just reaching for the key when something caught her eye. An animal was standing in the path beside the Doyles' cottage.

At first she wondered if one of the cows had got out— for a fir tree obscured her view. Then, as she went down the steps, she thought it might be a deer, standing so still, and walked quietly toward the path to avoid frightening it away.

Coming around the fir tree, Wendy caught her breath. It was a horse! But in such shocking condition that her heart stopped. Its hip bones stuck out sharp as elbows, its backbone was like the ridgepole of a tent, its withers raised in a hump, and each rib was plainly visible beneath the mangy fur.

"You poor thing! You're nothing but skin and bones!"

The horse tried to move. It was facing toward the stable, but seemed unable to go any further. Its coat was dry and dusty and dull, its tail and mane matted with burrs.

"How did you get here? Whose horse are you? Are you lost?"

The horse stretched its thin neck down toward the partially frozen ground and nosed weakly at the dried grass.

"Of course! You're hungry! Wait."

She ran to the stable and came back with a bucket of oats, which she set down before the horse. It raised its ears, moved its head toward the bucket, and hung over it, eyes half closed.

"Go ahead," Wendy urged. "What's the matter? Want me to go away?"

She went to sit upon the stone steps of the cottage, out of sight. Then, some moments later, when she saw the horse had not touched the oats, she brought it some bran mash instead. And then it occurred to her that the horse might be thirsty, and she brought up a bucket of water.

The horse had not touched the mash, either, but when she set down the water, it did drink, slowly. Wendy wondered where in the world the horse had come from. She knew all the horses from nearby stables, and could not imagine how this thin, ill-kept animal had got to Holiday Farm. Looking it over, she saw that in spite of its poor condition, it had well-shaped legs and a fine, tapering head. The eyes were large and set well apart. It was a mare, about the size of Lady.

Perhaps, she thought, when its thirst was quenched, the horse would eat something, and she pushed the mash invitingly close. Then, feeling the need of an older person's advice, she knocked on the kennelman's door.

"There's a stray horse out beyond the yard," she said.

"That so? I'll bet its owner is out looking for it."

"I don't know," Wendy said doubtfully. "She looks lost. I mean, more as if she didn't have an owner." Surely no owner would allow a horse to get in that condition, she thought. "She looks sick."

Jerry showed more interest. "Yeah? Let's have a look." Coming within sight of the mare, he said, "She does, at that. Keep her away from our horses. You don't know what's the matter, and even a cold is contagious."

"Isn't there something we can do for her?" Wendy asked.

Jerry walked back to his own house. "If Tim's away, that means you've got work to do, and so have I. I've got a sick pup here. But don't worry. The owner will show up. Horses are valuable. People don't just go off and forget them."

But perhaps, Wendy thought as the kennelman closed his door, that was just what had happened. Her owner might be away. She might have broken out and wandered away. But why? Horses loved the protection and food provided by the stable.

She went back to the mare, wondering what to do. She stood as before, head hanging near the bucket of food, not touching it. Her head swayed slightly now, and her eyes were dull. Wendy wished she could call the veterinarian, but she had no money for his bill and did not know if Mr. Holiday would pay for treatment of an animal not his own. Going into the Doyles' cottage, she telephoned her mother.

"Darling, I don't think you should do anything until Mr. Doyle comes back. He'll be home soon and will know what to do. And even if the horse is sick, another hour or so won't make any difference. Meanwhile, don't touch it. You haven't touched it, have you?"

". . . No." Wendy's answer was unconvincing.

"Then wash your hands with soap. You wouldn't want to give anything to the Holiday horses. Are you listening, Wendy?"

When she had washed her hands, Wendy went outside and found old Mr. Metcalf studying the animal. "A stray, huh? Ought to be ashamed, whoever owns her. It's a crime, letting an animal get in that condition."

"Do you think you ought to call Dr. Cronk?" she asked eagerly.

"Cronk?" The old man sniffed. "Know what he'd do?" The farmer cocked his finger toward the horse. "Bang! I had a friend had a couple of cows got sick. He called Cronk, and

Cronk came and shot the whole herd. He don't like animals, Cronk. But that animal ain't sick; it's starving."

Wendy clenched her fists, angry at herself and her own helplessness. Oh, why wasn't Tim there? Well, she had given the poor thing food and water; there was nothing else she could do. She changed her clothes, turned the ponies out in the yard, and made sure the yard gates were locked—just in case the stray did have something catching. But it wrung her heart, as she looked from Lady to the stray, to see the difference between them. Lady looked the way a mare should look, sleek and alert and beautiful. And as for Little Joe, whose big head gave him a babyish look, he was fat in comparison.

Wendy cleaned the stalls, rode each pony bareback in turn, and went to sit on the wall to look for the green Plymouth. But there was no sign of it. The lights came on in the Metcalfs' cottage and in Jerry Owen's, but still it did not come. Wendy wondered if something had happened to the Doyles' car. But if so, they would have telephoned. They knew she was there, waiting. At last, when it had been dark for some time, she plodded home.

After supper she called the Doyles' number, but there was no answer. Half an hour later she tried again, and the line was busy. She telephoned again and again, but their telephone was so consistently busy that she thought it must be out of order.

In the morning, before school, she telephoned again, and Marge answered. Wendy asked if they had seen the mare and if it were still there.

"We sure did, and it sure is!" Tim had been on the telephone all evening, trying to find its owner. "Looks like it's been wandering for weeks. It must have got out of a stable somewhere and got lost. I should think whoever owns it would be worried sick!"

That afternoon when the girls got to the farm, the mare had wandered to the side field and was standing among the weeds and tufts of grass that had been there all winter. Tim had thrown an old blanket over her during the night, but she looked no better.

Maureen felt sure the mare would eat for her, and had brought a carrot. But when she held it out, the mare just stood there. Wendy offered a piece of lump sugar. The horse nosed it, but when it fell to the ground, did not go after it. She stood as if too weak to care.

"Please try to eat something!" Wendy begged, and offered it again.

Maureen tried to thrust the sugar between the mare's teeth. "Look, dopey, you need nourishment. Sugar gives energy."

Tim came up behind them and pushed the girls away. "Let her be! How'd you like somebody forcing candy on you when you hadn't eaten for days?"

"What's she got? Is it catching?"

"No, she's just starving to death." Tim clenched his fists. "I'd like to get my hands on whoever owns her! I'd twist his neck like a dishrag. It's a crime, it is. A Federal crime. Did you know that, girls?"

They stroked her flea-bitten neck, but the mare seemed not to notice. Her eyes looked duller than before. The lids drooped. Wendy pulled burrs from the scraggly mane, but it seemed useless—there were so many.

"It's bad enough neglecting any horse," Tim stormed, "but imagine mistreating a thoroughbred!"

"She's a thoroughbred?" they asked in surprise.

"Can't you tell? Look at those straight, slender legs. Her lines are good even now, poor creature. And look here." He pulled back the mare's lips and showed them marks tattooed inside. "A race horse."

Besides the numbers tattooed inside her mouth, Tim had found the marks of a hypodermic needle on her hind legs. "They give them shots, you know, to strengthen the tendons."

"Do you think she'll—be all right—later?" Wendy asked.

"I do not! She's dying, I tell you. Dying of starvation."

"But can't you feed her somehow?"

Tim shook his head. "It's too late. She's too far gone. She's too weak. No, it's just a matter of time now, I'm afraid."

"She's going to *die?*" Maureen asked, unwilling to believe it.

"She's dying already. Dying on her feet. It would be a kindness to shoot her."

"You won't do that!" Wendy cried.

"No, it's not my job. I've called the state troopers. It's up to them to find the owner or else . . ."

When the girls walked home later that afternoon, they were buzzing with plans. They would go over early in the morning and make a liquid of warm bran mash. And if the mare would not take it by spoonfuls—well, they would make her. One of them would hold her mouth open—they were used to horses' teeth by now—and the other would put the food in.

"Then we'll hold her jaws closed so she has to swallow," Wendy said, remembering the time she and Steven had forced worm medicine down Patches' throat in this manner.

Before they reached Acorn Lake, their plans had gone even further. The mare not only would live, she would grow strong and well. They would groom her until she was sleek, and then—if no one claimed her—she would be their own— their very own horse! And if anyone did claim her—ha! They'd have the police on him!

Acorn Lake's rules about keeping animals melted away conveniently in Wendy's daydreams that evening, as she sat over her homework. She and Maureen kept the beautiful little mare—somewhere—and rode her and raced her. Forgotten was the fact that *one* horse between them would mean taking turns and riding alone. And that riding alone was no fun. They owned a race horse. . . .

The next day was Saturday, and Mr. Mason drove the girls to the farm. Tim had telephoned, asking him to come with his camera. The girls tumbled out of the car, eager to see their race horse. But when they saw her, their hopes collapsed. Her head hung lower than ever. Her coat looked more ragged than they had remembered. Her eyes looked lifeless.

"She's just waiting to die, poor thing," Tim said as Mr. Mason focused his camera and took pictures from several angles. "A heart-rending sight, isn't it? But I've called every horseman I know—and that's a good many—and none of them has any idea whose she can be. I even tried calling some I didn't know—and then I notified the police."

The troopers came while Mr. Mason and the girls were there. Neglect of horses was a misdemeanor, they said, according to Section 185 of the Penal Code, and subject to up to five hundred dollars' fine or imprisonment or both. However, they had no way of catching the criminal. They took down the numbers inside the mare's mouth, but since horses were sold and resold over and over again, it would be difficult to trace the owner.

"I don't think they're much interested," Tim complained when the troopers had gone. "They're too busy arresting people for speeding to care about dying horses."

A few moments later he came upon the girls, preparing their liquid mash, and shooed them away. "Can't you leave her alone? Can't you let the poor thing die in peace? Get along now, get out of my way."

They walked dejectedly down the driveway. They had

been determined that they would save the mare. Now Tim would not even let them try. At the main road Maureen turned right, toward Plumbridge, instead of left, toward Acorn Lake. "I'm going to the church. Want to come?"

Wendy nodded, and they walked to the village without speaking. But inside Wendy's head a chant seemed to beat. *She can't die. She can't. She won't die. She won't.*

Wendy had been to the Catholic church several times, twice with the O'Maras, and three or four times with the Doyles, but it still was strange to her. The dark interior, the painted statues, the ornate gold nave, altar, and icon, were very different from the Congregational church where she went to Sunday school, with its white walls, simple wooden altar, and bright stained-glass window showing Jesus holding a baby lamb.

Still, the very strangeness, the flickering candles and odor of incense, made the outside world seem far away. There was an air of quiet, a peace that was almost tangible.

Maureen had gone immediately to St. Francis, and placing a lighted candle before him, had begun to pray. Kneeling beside her, Wendy looked up at the figure before them. The saint's face had been carved into gentle lines, and his eyes painted with a kindly look. To Wendy, it was just a statue like any piece of sculpture, and meant no more than those she had seen in museums in New York. Nevertheless, she bowed her head and closed her eyes.

"Please don't let her die! Oh, don't let her die, you simply can't. You've got to let her live. Let her live!"

The quiet seemed to beat around her head, and Wendy suddenly wondered whether she had really been praying—or just demanding. Maureen rose, and they walked to the door. The air of quiet—and something else that Wendy could not name, something she could only feel inside her chest—was intense. They had pushed it aside, like a curtain, to come in, and now it was closing again behind them.

Mr. Mason was just leaving the farm as the girls returned. "I took some more pictures," he said, opening the door of the car for them. "Come on home. The little mare is dead, but I took some pictures of her lying there. The police will want them, I expect."

CHAPTER FOURTEEN

Bone Number Nineteen

"I said 'wash,'" Mrs. Mason said, looking sternly at Jamie. "Wash, or no popovers for you!"

"I did wash," Jamie protested, holding out his hands. "See?"

"You couldn't have—your face is all sticky."

"Well, gosh, you didn't say *face*; you just said, 'Wash your hands,'" Jamie grumbled on his way to the bathroom.

Wendy broke open a popover and buttered it.

"Why don't you eat paper napkins?" Steven asked her, buttering some toast for himself. "There's nothing to those things. Just empty shells."

"That's what I like about them," Wendy replied. "The empty shells."

She liked popovers at any time, but especially on a morning like this one, with streaks of sunshine slanting through the gray April sky. Easter Sunday had been cold, but now, only two days later, there was a touch of spring in the air.

She gave Patches a bit of her muffin and let him out. At the door she breathed deeply. Down in the lawn two yellow crocuses gleamed like fallen stars. A slight breeze stirred the willows. She wished she could go to the stable right now, instead of having to wait until after school. Yesterday they had begun schooling the horses for the coming shows. Tim had marked a course of jumps in the back field, setting up a "chicken coop," two brush jumps, and fences.

Sitting at her desk later, still thinking of yesterday's training program, Wendy drew a picture of the "in-and-out" jump Tim and Brendan had built. It was a pen made of four fences, just large enough for a horse to jump into and right out of again. Tim had taken both King and Vogue through this jump and today, he said, he was going to try Dan. Dan had wonderful possibilities, Wendy thought, if only he would obey Tim!

Miss Mitchell rapped with her pencil for attention. Now that it was spring, the whole class was unruly. One recreation period was not enough for their high spirits, it seemed. The teacher spoke rebukingly, but Wendy, for one, did not hear. She was thinking of a phrase that had come floating into her room from the television program her brothers had been watching the night before.

This here horse has got to be gentled 'fore I let you ride him, Miss June. You're much too young and pretty to be runnin' a ranch alone, anyways.

How were horses *gentled*, Wendy wondered, and could Dan be? An eraser hit her in the cheek, and without thinking she threw it back. Suddenly she realized Miss Mitchell was addressing her.

"Wendy, I *said* that the next person who threw an eraser would report to Dr. Low's office, and that did not excuse you. No, not now," she said as Wendy rose. "You may go at dismissal time."

At the dismissal bell Dr. Low told her to report to study hall and to go home on the second bus. So, for the second time, Tim and Maureen had already gone to the back field when Wendy arrived at the stable. She changed into her jodhpurs at the cottage, tacked up Little Joe, and rode to join them.

Maureen sat on a wall watching, as Tim took Dan over a fence.

"He's refused twice," she reported. "Tim's getting mad."

At the approach, Dan tried to run around the fence. Tim took him back, reined him around, and headed toward the jump. This time Dan took the jump, but as they were midway over, he jerked his head back, and it struck Tim on the chin.

"Are you all right, Mr. Doyle?" Wendy asked, as the groom rode back to where the girls were watching. "He hit you pretty hard."

"Sure, I'm all right," Tim said. He took the horse around the field once more, and this time Dan took the jump well, coming in at moderate speed, gathering up his forelegs, springing from strong hind legs, and keeping them well up. Tim was pleased.

"A few more times and I'll begin to feel I can count on him." Tim gave his head a shake, put a hand to his jaw, and added, "Maybe he's had enough for today, though. You kids give the ponies some schooling. I want to watch and see how they go."

The girls took turns riding over the complicated course Tim had marked out and outlined for them on paper. It was a figure eight inside the ring, with eight jumps in all, two of them brush fences, and in the center of the ring a "chicken coop"—an inverted V of wood. If they mastered it here at the farm, it would present no difficulty at the show grounds.

After an hour of this they walked the ponies home to the stable and stayed to clean the tack, while Tim went on to the cottage.

"What did you do to my boy friend?" Marge asked later when they came in to change their clothes. "He's all 'shook up.'"

"Nothing of the kind," said Tim. "I think I may be getting a bit of a cold, though."

"Yeah?" Marge said doubtfully. "I'd say you had a bad jolt. What really happened, kids?"

They told her how Dan's head had struck Tim's jaw. Tim began to laugh. "My *jaw* feels all right, but I'll be a sight to-morrow. What'll I tell the boss if he comes down and my chin's all black-and-blue?"

"Tell him Marge hit you." Maureen laughed.

"Say it's five-o'clock shadow," Wendy suggested. "Were you watching us? How did we do?" She had noticed that part of the time, at least, while they had schooled the ponies, Tim's eyes had been closed.

"Oh, not too badly," he said evasively. "You'll get on to it. Tomorrow's another day. But be here on time, Wendy. No more of this misbehaving in school and being kept after."

Brendan came in the room just in time to hear his father's remark. He shook his head at Wendy. "What? Not again!"

His words, so brotherlike, were food for thought. She would not let Steven tell on her again. So the first thing she said at supper was "I had to report to Dr. Low's office again today."

Her brother said not a word, and her father asked, "What for this time?" And when she admitted she had thrown an eraser, he remarked, "That sounds pretty babyish for a girl your age."

Nothing more was said about her misdemeanor, and Wendy decided she had better keep her mind on her classes after this.

The sun had turned her white window-blinds to yellow when Wendy opened her eyes. She blinked. It was morning, her door was closed, and no one was in her room. The feeling

she had that someone had been standing there must have been
a dream, she supposed. She washed, dressed, and went to
breakfast, wondering if today Tim might let her and Maureen try the in-and-out jump. But I mustn't think about it
during school, she reminded herself.

After breakfast, when she went to her room for her books
and coat, she again remembered that feeling that someone had
been there. Then, over her desk, she noticed a change. In the
pine frame on the wall, which had always held a picture of a
young colt, was a photograph of a man. How did that get
there, she wondered. It looked just like Dr. Low.

"It *is* Dr. Low," Steven said, poking his head into the room.
"Like it?"

Wendy opened and closed her mouth like a fish on a hook.
"Where did it come from?"

He shrugged. "From an old yearbook. I thought since
you're so crazy about the guy that you have to visit him all
the time . . ."

Wendy giggled and hit at him with one of her books.
"Thanks, pal."

"Better keep out of Tim's way today," Marge warned as
the girls came into the cottage that afternoon for their jodhpurs.

"Why, is he in a bad mood?" Maureen was always more
outspoken than Wendy would have dared be.

Marge considered. "I don't know. To tell you the truth,
that blow he got from Dan yesterday shook him up more
than he realizes."

"Okay, we'll be careful."

The in-and-out jump was set up in the field. Tim had been
schooling Dan over the stone wall and over brush jumps and
now he was ready to try him on the in-and-out.

"You're just in time," he called. "I want you kids to watch and tell me how he looks." He dug his heels into Dan's sides, took him from a trot into a canter, and then into a hard gallop toward the jump. Dan's hoofs thundered toward the pen.

There was a shout and a thud. Tim had toppled off the horse. The girls rushed forward and climbed the fence. Tim was lying inside the pen, still and white, the reins clasped in his hands. Dan stood quietly beside him. Shocked and amazed, the girls waited for Tim to regain consciousness, as he had done in the stable long ago, but when after a few minutes that seemed like hours he had not stirred, they became alarmed.

Maureen knelt and took hold of his shoulder. "Mr. Doyle! Mr. Doyle!"

"What shall we do?" Wendy cried.

"I'd better go get Marge or somebody," Maureen said.

"Wait a minute."

Tim's eyelids were fluttering. Then his eyes opened, and with a groan he tried to sit up.

"You'd better lie still," Wendy told him. "You had a bad fall."

Tim shook his head as if to clear it and passed a hand over his eyes. Then he saw the reins in his other hand and realized what had happened. He looked up at the horse and got to his feet.

"Get out, kids," he ordered. "You heard me—out!" he shouted, when neither of them moved. "Get the devil out of this jump!"

"Why? What are you going to do?" Wendy asked.

"I'm going to give this idiot the beating of his life and then I'm going to take him through that jump." Tim reached for the crop that had fallen to the ground, but Maureen got it first.

"No, you're not going to beat him. It wasn't Dan's fault. You just fell off."

"I *what?*" Tim roared.

"You did. Honest, Mr. Doyle. I think you must have been shaky from that blow you got yesterday and blacked out for a second."

"Yes, that's what it looked like," Wendy agreed.

"Give me that crop, blast you!" Tim said, advancing on Maureen. "I'm going to . . ."

His knees buckled, and the girls rushed to catch hold of him and help him to the fence.

"I'm all right," he insisted. "Let go of me! Can't you see I've got to show that blasted animal who's boss? If I don't, he'll be no good to me or anyone."

Tim was deathly pale, and his whole body was shaking.

"You're not going to get on that horse," Maureen insisted.

"Get out of my way." Tim took a faltering step from the fence. Wendy grabbed his arm, and together she and Maureen pried the reins from his hand. Tim, weakened by his fall, could do nothing but rant at them. Then he grew dizzy, reached out blindly for the rail fence, sank to his knees, and fainted.

Wendy whipped off her jacket and put it under his head. Maureen put hers over his chest and shoulders. Together the girls lifted down one of the top rails, and Maureen led Dan out of the jump.

"You stay with Tim. I'll take Dan back to the stable and come back with Marge." Maureen got into the saddle. "Don't let him get up or anything," she called back as she rode off. "Don't stand for any nonsense."

By the time Marge and Jerry arrived, Tim was conscious and asked Jerry to help him up.

"Better not, Tim," Jerry said. "You don't know what's broken."

"Take it easy, Tim," Marge advised. "Dr. Clarke is on the way."

"Oh, come on. I feel like a fool, lying on the ground with women and children standing about. Come, Jerry, give me a hand."

"I'll give you my foot!" Marge snapped. "You lie still and be quiet!" She knelt beside him suddenly and felt his forehead. "Oh, Tim. I hope you're all right."

Seeing the doctor's car approach on the lane, the girls ran to move the gate so he could drive into the field through a gap in the stone wall.

"Well, Tim," Dr. Clarke said, "what have you done to yourself this time?" He examined him quickly.

"Nothing," Tim answered weakly, "compared with what I'm going to do to that stubborn nag tomorrow when I'm up to it."

"It won't be tomorrow, I'm afraid," the doctor stated as an ambulance came through the gap and pulled up nearby.

Tim tried to look around. "Eh? What's this, now? Where are you taking me?"

Instead of answering, the doctor and the ambulance driver lifted Tim onto a stretcher and covered him with blankets. The stretcher was put inside, and Marge was shown where she might sit beside the stretcher. Then the ambulance followed the doctor's car out of the field.

"I wonder what he's broken this time," Jerry Owen mused.

"Bone number nineteen," Maureen answered.

CHAPTER FIFTEEN

Wendy Pays a Call

Marge Doyle telephoned that evening. Tim had a bad concussion and several bruises, but no broken bones. He would have to stay in the hospital, however, for at least ten days, and she wondered if Wendy and Maureen could come over and help with the horses.

"Why, of *course!*" Wendy was surprised that Marge would even ask.

"Thank you. We'd appreciate it. And Mr. Holiday will, too."

Marge did not sound like herself, thanking them formally as if they were outsiders. Marge ought to have known they would come without being asked, and that they needed no thanks. But then, Wendy realized, nobody ever sounded natural when troubled.

So once more the "stableboys" were in charge of the five Holiday horses, as they had been during Tim's vacation. The big difference was that now school was on, they had to get up at five to do the morning work at the stable. Before getting on the school bus, they must take the soiled straw out of the stalls, turn the horses out in the field, and fill water pails and oats buckets.

After school they got off the bus at the farm, changed their clothes, exercised the horses, and put them in again. To save

xtra work they again rode bareback, putting only halters and
eads on the ponies.

Marge made them promise not to try anything new until
Tim came home.

"I have enough to worry about without worrying about
you two."

They promised not even to jump.

Marge went to the hospital afternoons, and again in the
evenings with Brendan, taking messages from the girls and
bringing word from Tim. He was getting along well except
for the severe headaches from the concussion, but he was
relieved to know the girls were doing his job for him, he said.

"Tell him Dan took an apple from Wendy without biting
her," Maureen said, hanging to the car as Marge left one day.
"And tell him to hurry home. We're dying to try the in-and-
out."

"Yes, and tell him Little Joe says hello," Wendy called.
"And ask him if it's all right for King to have extra oats, now
he's not working. He always seems to be looking for more."

The messages from Tim to his stableboys became so
numerous that Marge spent almost all the visiting hour writing them down.

"I wish we could see him." Wendy sighed.

"I wish you could too," Marge said. "I know Tim would
love to see you. I tell him the horses are all right, and Brendan
tells him, but he still worries. It's not like hearing about it from
his stableboys!"

"We'll go, then!" Maureen stated. "Why shouldn't we?"

"Hospital rules. No children under fifteen allowed as visitors."

"Heck! I'll be fifteen in the fall!"

"They might let you in then," Marge said. "I could ask. But
they probably have to stick close to the rules."

"Rules again. Rules, rules, rules," Wendy chanted.

"Let's go anyway," Maureen said rebelliously as she walked home with Wendy. "We'll just walk in! They can't stop us!"

"They'd stop *me*." Wendy sighed. "But you could easily pass for fifteen, even though most kids fifteen wear lipstick. At least you're tall."

"Wendy!" Maureen cried, her eyes lighting up with mischief. "That's it! That's what we'll do. What do you say? Are you game?"

Mr. and Mrs. Mason had taken Jamie to an early movie when Maureen came over that evening. She was wearing her mother's high-heeled shoes, and lipstick was generously applied to her lips. Mrs. Mason's shoes were much too big for Wendy, however, and she could not walk in them at all.

"Going to a costume party as a lady clown?" Steven asked as she came in.

"Hey, Steve, be a good kid and run next door and ask Debbie Lewis for some shoes. She has those little heels."

"You kids look about as grown up as two five-year-olds playing lady," he commented sourly as he went reluctantly to borrow shoes from the high-school girl next door.

When he returned, he had hats and earrings for good measure, and the girls carried them and the shoes, along with compacts and lipsticks, to the Doyles' cottage.

When Marge saw them, she lay down on the sofa and buried her face in a pillow. After a moment she dried her eyes and gave them some cold cream.

"When you get old enough to use lipstick," she said, "I hope somebody will show you how to put it on properly."

After their faces had been cleaned with both cold cream and soap and water, Marge dusted their noses lightly with powder and put just a faint trace of lipstick on their lips.

"How do we look?" Wendy asked.

Marge stood back and nodded appreciatively. They looked o different from the two girls who worked in the stable as o be almost unrecognizable. They were wearing their best unday dresses and nylon stockings. Maureen's dark curls were eld back with a green ribbon. Wendy's pigtails were un- one, and her hair waved softly over her shoulders.

"You look like a pair of angels!" Marge marveled. "I can't elieve it."

"Do you think we'll get in at the hospital?" Maureen asked.

Marge smiled mysteriously. "I wouldn't be surprised."

The girls giggled all the way to Mount Kisco, but when Marge drove up to the big red brick building and parked the ar, they grew quiet and nervous. They walked through the vhite-pillared entrance, not even daring to speak.

"You wait here," Marge told them, and went to speak to he nurse at the desk. After a few minutes she returned with hree visitors' cards.

"We made it!" Maureen cried, wrinkling her nose with leasure.

"Be quiet," Marge warned, "or they may put you out."

Marge led the way to the elevators. The door closed, and he elevator moved upward very slowly. At the third floor it topped, the door opened, and a nurse was waiting with a small oy in a wheel chair. Down the hall, walking at a snail's pace nd steadying herself by holding to the wall, came a very old ady in a robe.

Odors of medicine, disinfectant, and anesthetic mingled with those of food and floor polish. Wendy heard a clatter of dishes s an orderly pushed a cart loaded with trays down a corri- dor. A voice over a loudspeaker said, "Dr. Thayer wanted n surgery." And a shiver went up her back.

Most of the doors they passed were closed, but through on that was ajar Wendy caught sight of a man swathed in band ages. She shuddered, hoping Tim would not look like that.

As they passed the hall desk, a nurse's cap was just visibl above the switchboard. Her head was bent, and she seeme not to see them.

"Have you visitors' cards?" Her voice stopped them.

Marge showed her the cards.

"No children allowed."

The girls' faces fell with disappointment.

"I'm *practically* . . ." Maureen began, but Marge wa speaking.

"I have special permission from Dr. Clarke to let thes girls see Mr. Doyle. I talked to him on the phone this morning and he agreed Mr. Doyle might not be so restless if he coul talk to them. The doctor left word at the desk downstairs."

The girls looked at her in surprise. "Did you really ge special permission?" Maureen asked as the nurse checked witl the main desk. "Why didn't you tell us?"

Marge could not help laughing. "I didn't want to spoil you fun. You were enjoying your—disguises so much!"

"All right. You may go in," the nurse said. "But don't stay too long."

Tim was lying in a high bed with a bandage around his fore head. His ruddy, weather-beaten face looked out of plac against the white pillows, and the lower part of his neck which showed above the hospital shirt, looked strangely white But his eyes looked bluer than ever, and his eyebrows more than ever like bits of straw brought in from the stable.

"Hello, Marge," he said wearily. Then he saw the girls They came closer, grinning. He took a better look. "Are thes my stableboys? These two beautiful young ladies?"

"How do you feel?" Wendy asked.

"Like a million, if they'd just let me out of here. You'd think I had nothing to do. I don't know why they're keeping me in bed, and that's the truth. I've had worse spills than that one, and not been laid up and pampered like this, like one of Jerry's poodles! Why, I remember one time, when I was working for Mr. Emmet Phillips in Westport . . ."

"Tim, you're not supposed to talk much," Marge reminded him.

He subsided with a sigh. "Everybody keeps giving me orders."

"You sound fine," Maureen said. "Just like yourself. Next thing, you'll be swearing at us."

He looked surprised. "I don't swear at you, do I? Not often, surely. Only when something's gone wrong and my temper's raggedy. Well, how's everything at the stable? How are old King and Vogue? What about the ponies?"

"They're all fine," Wendy assured him.

"Except Dan. He's brokenhearted that you're away," Maureen said mischievously.

Tim turned his head on the pillow. "Ah, Dan. Dan, that scoundrel. There's only one thing wrong with me, girls. And that's right here." He thumped a fist against his heart. "I'm sick at heart over old Dan. Poor fellow. I thought I could do something with him, make a fine hunter out of him, but now the boss wants to get rid of him."

A stout nurse bustled in with a thermometer. She looked sharply at the girls, as she thrust the thermometer into her patient's mouth. "You girls will have to wait downstairs in the lounge. Good evening, Mrs. Doyle," she added with a disapproving nod at Marge.

Tim smiled at them around the thermometer, winked, and waved a hand.

*

On the way home Marge was so quiet that the girls wondered if she was worried about Tim.

"No, he's coming along all right. I was just thinking about Dan. As soon as he heard of the accident, Mr. Holiday said he was going to sell him. But with Tim landing in the hospital —well, you know how word gets around. Everybody started saying that if Tim couldn't handle Dan, nobody could. And now Mr. Holiday will never get a buyer for him. We didn't tell Tim, but I guess he's figured it out for himself. No wonder he's heartsick. He always hates to think of a sound horse being put down."

"You mean shot?" Maureen cried. "They wouldn't shoot Dan!"

"Not if they can find a buyer. But who'd buy him—a horse that's dangerous? If he'd throw Tim . . ." The lighted windows of a drugstore gleamed in the dark village. "You kids want a soda?"

A moment before, they would have said yes. Now neither girl was interested. "Dan's a swell horse, even if he is mean. And a good jumper. I'll bet lots of people would be glad to buy him," Maureen said.

"Who, for instance?" Marge asked. "Dan had a bad reputation when they bought him, but Tim thought he could handle him. You know what gossips professional horsemen are. If word gets around that a man with Tim's experience couldn't handle him, who'd want to hunt him?"

At the railroad crossing ahead the lights blinked red from side to side, and Marge stopped. The gate came down.

"But he'd make a good hunter," Wendy insisted. "He may not jump the way Mr. Doyle wants him to, but he can jump, all right! Look at the way he jumped the yard wall! But *he* wants him to be *perfect*. It's like my parents with my brother Jamie. They don't expect him to be as tall as Steven, because he's so much younger, but they expect him to have as much sense."

They sat silent for a moment as the distant gleam of the single light came closer, growing from flashlight size to a great, blinding headlight. The train hissed to a stop, and the smell of oil from the diesel engine came through the closed windows of the car. Wendy looked at the people sitting by the windows and wondered where they were going. The people looked briefly at them. Then the engine hummed and throbbed and roared, and the faces ran together like a water color that is too wet, and the train slid by in a blur of light.

"It's hard," Marge said, "not to want perfection from those you've brought up yourself, to let them jump—or go—their own way. They mean more to you because they're your own. You've raised them and you're so darned eager for them to turn out right that you're not fair to them. You don't even notice that they might have a good way of going of their own."

When Marge dropped the girls at Acorn Lake, there was a fine mist in the air. The girls stood silent, their thoughts close.

"Good we decided to put the ponies in."

"Yeah."

"Why would anybody shoot a swell horse like Dan?"

Wendy sighed deeply, remembering Tim's story of having to shoot his own hunter, remembering the stray race-horse. "Well, see you tomorrow."

"Yeah. See you."

The living room was dark except for the light of the television set. The Outrider was just dusting off his ten-gallon hat as Wendy walked in. A stagecoach rolled by, and a pretty girl waved from its window. The Outrider gave a wry smile, shrugged, and sauntered off on his high-heeled boots, whistling for his horse. Then, as the theme music came on, Steven switched off the set.

"Well, how'd it go?" He turned on a light. "Anybody mistake you for Mr. Doyle's grandmother?"

Wendy suddenly felt depressed. "Where are Mom and Dad?"

"Out."

"Steve," she burst out, wanting to relieve the heaviness in her heart by talking to someone. "You know Dan, the horse that threw Tim? Mr. Holiday is going to have him put down. He's got good lines and he's a good jumper, but they're going to have him shot. Unless somebody buys him."

Steven put a hand in his pocket. "I can let you have about thirty-five cents."

"Oh, Steven! I just mean—isn't it awful—the idea of taking a beautiful animal like that, strong and full of life and . . . and . . ."

Steven rolled over on his back and yawned. "Don't tell *me* about it. Go tell Mr. Holiday."

She had asked for sympathy, and he had responded with indifference. Wendy looked at her brother with rage. "You! What do you care? All you care about is movie horses ridden by cowboys who are really only actors! Don't you care about real horses at all?"

She stamped down the hall into her room and slammed the door. For a few minutes there was silence in the living room, as if Steven had been stunned by her outburst. Then she heard him come down the hall and stop outside her door.

"Wendy. What I meant was . . ."

"Go away! You and your old television programs!" She threw her shoe at the door. Steven waited until she had thrown the other one, then he opened the door. She was sprawled face down upon the bed.

"What I meant was if you care so much, why don't you do something about it? Go talk to Mr. Holiday."

"Oh, sure! He'd listen to me!"

"He might. It's like this show I saw the other night on. . . . Wait a minute," he said as she turned her head away in disgust. "I don't only watch Westerns. The other night I saw this movie about this guy Zola. He wrote a letter to the King of France, bawling him out. He wasn't anybody, this Zola, just a writer or something, but they'd arrested this guy Dreyfus, who wasn't really guilty. Zola didn't even know the guy, but he was in prison, and when they didn't let him out even after another guy had confessed, Zola got sore. So he wrote the King, or President of France or whoever he was, and told him just what he thought of his crummy idea of justice. Well, it's the same thing, isn't it?"

Wendy got up with a sigh and pulled down her bedspread. "Beat it, will you? I'm tired."

But later, when she was lying awake, it occurred to her that Steven might be right. She could at least ask Mr. Holiday to wait a while. Maybe she and Maureen could find a buyer for Dan. . . .

Her clock ticked loudly, and tree toads went *per-whee, per-whee*, and she felt as wide awake as if it were afternoon. The wind came up. It rustled through the trees and clattered the window blind, and she could hear little wavelets slapping against the canoe.

She rehearsed her appeal to Mr. Holiday. "Please, won't you give Dan a chance . . .?"

When Maureen came down her back steps in answer to Wendy's knock the next morning, the younger girl told of her plan to talk to Mr. Holiday. In the night Wendy had resolved to go up to the big house herself, acting with as much courage as Zola. But in the morning it had seemed that writing a letter was one thing; going right up to a person—especially one who had let you ride his horses and who had paid your entrance fees at horse shows and your capping fees at hunts—was another. And there was not time to write a letter. If Maureen were along, though . . .

"You go," Maureen said. "I'm going in to Plumbridge." She looked down at the road as they walked to the farm. "I'm going to stop in at the church. I talked to Father Shea—after the last time when the mare died—and he said I was being willful. This time—I won't be."

"Okay. I'll see you later, then."

They walked together past the gravel driveway leading to the stable, down the main road to the entrance to the other driveway—smooth and winding—that led to the big house on the hill. Wendy waved to Maureen and walked through the wrought-iron gate with the words "Holiday Farm" in scrollwork overhead.

She felt butterflies in her stomach as she walked past the formal planting at both sides of the gate. She tried to remember the brave words she had rehearsed the night before, but in broad daylight they seemed ridiculous. The big house itself was not even in sight as she trudged along the pavement with gutters on both sides that Marge said had cost thousands and thousands of dollars. Her veins felt as if they were filled with ice water, and her heart seemed caught between her ribs, going *bump, bump, bump.*

Up the hill she saw hundreds of daffodils, set in clumps here and there as if by accident. Overhead, poplars twinkled their little leaves, holding them carelessly by threadlike stems, so that they spun and sparkled.

It was a long walk. Wendy passed the empty swimming pool—the shape and color of a robin's egg—the red clay tennis courts, the garden in which a wrinkled man whom she knew from the farm garden was working. He looked up and smiled. Several cars were parked in the paved area before the house, and Wendy's heart expanded a little. If he has company, I'd better not bother him, she thought.

She turned to go back. "Coward! You know that's just an excuse," a voice inside her accused. She sighed, and turned again to the house.

Outside the door there was a funny sort of bell, like one she had seen on a picture of an old mission. She pulled the cord, but could hear nothing. A moment later, however, the heavy door was opened by a gray-haired man wearing striped trousers and a cutaway coat.

"Yes, miss?" She had heard that the Holidays had a butler but had not really believed it.

"Is Mr. Holiday at home?"

"I'll see. Who is calling?"

Before she could answer, Mr. Holiday himself came down the hall. "Hello, Wendy. What can I do for you?"

The moment had come. Wendy's heart seemed to have stopped. But Mr. Holiday was waiting, and in a business suit he did not look very different from Mr. O'Mara or friends of her father's.

"I came to ask you—please don't have Dan put down. He's a peach of a horse. I don't know if you've ridden him, but Maureen and I have. We've exercised him for Tim with the others. He's really not bad."

Mr. Holiday smiled. "You're very loyal to the Holiday horses, I know. But you see, Wendy, I trust Tim's judgment, and if he can't make a hunter out of a horse, then that horse is no use to me. I'm interested in horse shows, but only to a degree. My real interest is in hunting. Every man has his sport. Your father, perhaps, plays golf. I . . ."

"Tennis," she said, "and skating." Looking past him, she saw a wide hall and, unbelievably, a row of suits of armor.

"My only reason for buying Dan," Mr. Holiday went on, "was to have a hunter for my guests. I could hardly put a friend on Dan, when he's shown himself to be so dangerous. Tim was lucky, you know. A less capable rider would have been killed."

Wendy nodded. He was right, she supposed. "But you don't have to shoot him."

"I'd much prefer selling him. But who will buy him now? Everyone has heard of Tim's accident." He looked down at her woebegone face a moment. "I tell you what. If I can't find a buyer, I'll give him away. How's that?"

Wendy nodded again and turned away, remembering to thank him.

Well, that was that. That was what she had come for, wasn't it? She kicked a pebble along the drive. "Mission accomplished," she said aloud.

Then why did she feel a vague dissatisfaction?

CHAPTER SIXTEEN
Wendy Sets a Trap

Sunlight dappled Little Joe's neck and Lady's rump as Wendy and Maureen circled the back field. Apple trees dotted the neighboring hills with shimmering pink, and dogwood brightened the banks of Lundy Lane. It was a day of humming insects, of bird song—a wonderful day to be riding.

They were not allowed to jump until Tim came, and Maureen suggested they go exploring through the woods rather than practice posting on the diagonal as he had suggested.

"But he said he would be right up," Wendy said.

"Pooh! They'll be talking for another hour. At least Tim will."

Bert Buchanan had stopped by to talk about the P.H.A. show. Tim, after ten days in the hospital and another week's rest at home, was strong and well and back at work.

Wendy was about to suggest that they take the course once before exploring, when she noticed a truck parked on the lane. "Who's that?"

They rode over to see. Coming closer, they saw that the truck was stuck, its back wheel in the ditch. The driver, a short, swarthy man in a soiled shirt, looked up defensively.

"What's the matter—is it a private road or something? It ain't marked."

"No, it's not private." Maureen followed his glance to the

"Posted" signs tacked to the trees. "Those signs mean *this* property—Holiday's—but it only goes as far as the lane."

"Holiday's?"

"Carter Holiday. He owns all the way from here to the main road."

The man kicked at the truck tire. "Well, if it ain't private, it's a wonder the town don't take care of it. I'll never get that wheel out. Is there a garage around here?"

"There's one in Plumbridge. That's three miles," Wendy told him.

He ran a finger back and forth under his nose. "You kids do much riding around in there?" He jerked his head toward the fields.

"Mostly in the jump course. Why?" Maureen asked.

"Nothing. I just—I wondered if you could phone up that garage for me. I got to get out of here."

Wendy wondered what was in the truck, a battered-looking one. Riding around to the back, she read: ANTHONY FARRO —JUNK. She did not like the man, but she supposed they might as well help him. "We'll call Powell's."

As they were starting off, they heard hoofbeats. Tim was coming down Lundy Lane on King. Apparently Bert Buchanan had left right away. Seeing the truck, Tim slowed King to a walk, and the girls rode back, for surely Tim would be able to help.

"Morning, neighbor. In trouble?" Tim was asking.

Wendy noticed something odd. The gate that usually closed the gap in the stone wall was open. They had opened it the day of Tim's accident, but Jerry Owen had closed it after the ambulance.

"Maybe *he* opened it," Maureen said, nodding toward the truckman. "Probably coming in to look for a house to phone from."

"The dope. Couldn't he climb?"

Tim was calling them. "Wendy! *Maur*een! Ride to the farm and see if Jerry's there and tell him to bring up the truck and a heavy rope. No need to call a tow truck," he said to the driver. "We'll get you out."

"Some road!" the truckman grumbled. "You could break an axle in that ditch."

Tim said that he had been over the road hundreds of times without noticing it. But then, he had always been on horseback. The road was narrow and not used much by cars.

The girls had obediently turned their ponies to head back to the farm, but, once out of sight, Maureen, instead of heading toward the path, rode to the second field.

"Hey, where are you going?"

"Just taking a long cut. Why should we hurry for him? I'll bet he's got stolen goods in that truck. Notice how sneaky he was?"

Wendy giggled. "Maybe we better not help him, then. We don't want to be caught 'aiding and abetting' a criminal."

They rode side by side through a field grown high with grasses and wild flowers, and coming to a little fir tree, passed on either side of it saying, "Bread and butter."

Then Little Joe shied. Wendy grabbed his mane to steady herself. The pony's ears were laid back, and he wanted to run, but she held him. "What's the matter, boy?" And then she saw what it was that had frightened him. In the shadow of the fir, half hidden by a clump of sumac, stood a horse without halter or bridle.

"Maureen! Come here quick!"

Maureen rode over. The horse was in the same pitiful condition as the stray that had wandered to the farm earlier that spring. It was as if they were seeing a ghost. Its head sagged over the long grass. The jutting jawbone, the long, thin neck, the ribs as clearly defined as those of animal skeletons in the Museum of Natural History, made it a twin—except in color —of the race horse that had died.

Maureen shuddered. "Let's go." She headed Lady toward the path, and Little Joe followed.

"How did it get in here?" Wendy whispered. It seemed wrong to speak aloud with the mare standing there like a specter.

"How did the other one get in?" There was an edge of anger to Maureen's voice. "The gate's always closed, and Tim said it wasn't a jumper, so they must have . . ." Looking at the ground for hoofprints, she saw something else.

"Tire marks," Wendy exclaimed. "Truck tires. Why, our truck never . . ."

She caught her breath and looked from the marks in the field to the truck on Lundy Lane.

Maureen's eyes narrowed. "He wanted us to telephone? We'll telephone, all right! Come on, Wendy!" In another moment she pulled Lady up, waiting for Wendy to come alongside. "No! We can't! Tim's working with him. They might get it out, and then he'll get away."

"That's right. Or somebody might come along and give him a push."

"I'll go telephone," Maureen said. "You go back and keep him there." And she rode off.

"How?" Wendy called, but Maureen was already on the path. Of course, Wendy thought, riding back, I'll just tell Tim what we found.

But when she got back, Tim had tied King to a tree in the field, and he and the truckman were busy pushing a board under the wheel. "Not now, I'm busy," Tim replied, when she asked to speak to him for a moment.

"But it's important. I want to show you something."

The truck driver looked up quickly and gave her a suspicious glare, and Wendy was almost glad Tim was busy; if he left, the truckman might just run away.

"I told you kids to go for help," Tim said from the ditch.

"Maureen *has* gone for help," Wendy replied, and slipping out of the saddle, she tied Little Joe beside King and slid down the bank to the road. By now they had the board in front of the wheel. The driver got into the cab and started the motor. Wendy took the opportunity to beckon wildly to Tim.

"Out of the way," he said, going to the back of the truck. "You'll get hurt." The driver pressed the gas pedal, and Tim put his shoulder against the back of the truck.

"*Stop!*" Wendy shouted. "You can't do that!" She ran to the front of the truck and climbed up to shout above the noise of the motor. "Don't let him push! He's just come out of the hospital!"

The driver looked around at Tim. "No fooling, Mac? You just out of the hospital? Why didn't you say so?"

Tim insisted he was all right. "A little shove won't hurt me. Come on, I think we can get her out."

Wendy shook her fists at him, now more concerned over Tim than over the driver's possible escape. "You big boob! What would Marge say?"

The driver turned off the motor. "Nothing doing. That other kid's gone for help. I can wait."

Wendy gave a great sigh of relief, but in another moment she was gasping with chagrin. Tim was walking to the front of the truck.

"Hop down, man. I'll take the wheel; you push. You're huskier than I am, anyway." He got into the seat and studied the dashboard.

The truckman put a strong shoulder against the truck and pushed as the motor started. It did not budge. He took a deep breath, his eyes closing tight, his face squeezed into a grimace. "*Ooogh!*" This time the wheel went up onto the board and out onto firm ground.

"Okay!" Tim shouted. "She's out."

Wendy watched in dismay. The truck was free. The driver would go away, and they had wanted to catch him red-handed. She bit at her knuckle. If only she could think of some way to keep him captive until Jerry came with the police! For surely they were on the way!

Something clicked in her mind. *Captive*. What was that phrase Marge had used one day—captive audience? "*He's a captive audience. Caught like a rabbit in a trap.*"

The driver was walking to the front of the truck. "Much obliged. Hope you didn't strain your heart none pushing."

Tim had stopped to light a cigarette. "Oh, the old ticker's strong enough. It was a concussion I had." He put one foot out of the cab.

"How it happened, he had been riding Dan, this stubborn horse we have, the day before," Wendy prompted breathlessly, "and Dan's head hit him, and he was shaky, so . . ."

"I was *not* shaky, Miss Mason," Tim said, turning to face her as she climbed into the cab beside him, "I'll thank you to remember. I've told you girls that, and I've told Marge countless times."

At least, Wendy thought, sighing, I've got him started.

"It takes more than a little nudge like that to shake me. I've had blows enough, the good Lord knows, to stand a whack on the chin like that one."

The driver stood ready to get into the cab as soon as Tim got down, but Tim, holding to the wheel, was nodding thoughtfully. "Dan's a bad actor, all right, but it wasn't that. I had a bit of a cold that day, as I remember. I was weary, I guess. My old bones ached and my temper was raggedy. So it could have been that . . ."

Wendy went around to the back of the truck and wrote the license number in the dirt with a stick—just in case the man got away before help came. When she got back, Tim was describing his accident step by step in detail with all the events leading up to it. The driver cleared his throat nervously from time to time as if to interrupt. Wendy smiled. She knew it was no use.

Several times the man did get in a "Well, I . . ." or a "Look, Mac," but each time Tim went on in his unhurried way. ". . . know as well as I do a horse that won't take orders when it's young is spoiled for life. 'No,' I said, 'No, by the saints, you're going to take that jump if I have to stay here all night. And what's more, you'll take it as I want you to.' So back we went for another try."

The truckman raised his hand. "Maybe I'd better be . . ."

"Ordinarily I don't use a crop, see, but this time I let old Dan feel it." Wendy wandered down the road a few steps, listening for the sound of a car, and hearing none, came back. Tim had got to the place in his story where he had been taken to the hospital.

". . . and here I am, alive to tell the tale," Tim said, concluding his story.

Wendy recognized the sound of finality. Why, today of all days, did Tim have to stop talking? And what was taking Jerry so long?

"It was your own fault you were hurt," she put in quickly. "Mr. Holiday wouldn't have bought Dan except for your saying so."

"You're right there," Tim admitted. "I liked the look of him. Ah, well, all water under the dam." Another note of finality.

"Much obliged," the driver said again. "Now, I'll be getting on."

"Mr. Doyle's usually right about horses, though," Wendy told him. "Like the time Mr. Phillips wanted to buy this . . ."

"You've heard of Mr. Emmet Phillips of Westport?" Tim asked. "You must have, having a Connecticut license. Loaded with money, the man was, one of the wealthiest men in the state. And wouldn't you think a man with a fine education like that would know better? Ordinarily he took me along, you know, when he wanted a new horse. But this time, off he goes on his own and comes back with this nag. Paid a pretty penny for him too, you may be sure."

"If you don't mind, buddy . . ." the driver said, growing impatient.

"You never saw such a creature in your life! 'You can just take him back where he came from,' I said."

The driver stepped up, glaring at the groom. "Okay, okay . . ."

"I could see at a glance," Tim continued, "he had everything wrong with him a horse can have: over in the knee, mutton-withered . . ."

The driver leaned in threateningly. "*Listen!* I ain't got time to stand around all day!"

A car was coming up the road. Wendy recognized the cough of the motor and the rattle of the loose bumper. "Hurray!"

"Well, here's the old Plymouth," Tim observed, getting down from the cab. "I guess Jerry wasn't there. Hello, Marge," he said, seeing his wife at the wheel. "You're too late. We got it out without you."

"Oh, no I'm not!" Marge replied. A police car pulled from behind her to stop in front of the truck, blocking its escape.

"Hello, Frank. What's up?" Tim asked as a trooper got out.

"Mrs. Doyle says somebody dumped another sick horse back here. Is this the guy?"

And now, coming from the other direction on Lundy Lane, the farm truck chugged up with Mrs. Metcalf at the wheel, Jerry Owen beside her. Then everyone was talking at once—Tim expressing his astonishment, the girls offering to show where the horse stood hidden by the fir tree, the others asking questions.

"Another mare!" Tim exclaimed, when the girls had taken him to the spot in the second field where they had found her. "Just like the other."

The mare was no longer standing beside the fir. She was lying quite still. Lying there in the long grass, one foreleg crossed over the other, she might have been sleeping.

"Starved to death," Tim pronounced. "Just like the first one." He examined her mouth and found similar marks. "Another old race horse."

Frank Regan, the trooper, was comparing the tire marks in the field with those in the gap and on the road directly behind the truck.

"I don't know nothing about it—honest!" the driver protested. "I was only following orders."

"Whose orders?" the trooper asked.

"My boss—Farro. I didn't have nothing to do with it. I didn't know if they were sick or not. All I know is, I do what he tells me."

"And he told you to drive over the state line, did he, and dump them in New York?"

The driver shrugged. "He's the boss. I do what he says. He says he can't afford to feed them no more; I should take them someplace where there's grass."

"There was no grass last time!" Tim thundered. "Only March it was, when that first poor creature was dumped here.

Where's your common decency, man, letting an animal starve like that?"

The trooper ordered the driver to come to headquarters for questioning.

"What for? What's the charge?"

"Misdemeanor. Section 185 of the Penal Code. Willful neglect of an animal. Leave the truck here."

"Gee, I don't like to do that," the driver protested. "I'll get in trouble with Farro."

"You're in plenty of trouble now." The trooper laughed humorlessly. "And so's Farro!"

The trooper called Tim that evening while the girls were having supper with the Doyles.

"He did, eh?" they heard Tim say. "Well, no punishment is too stiff for him. The driver, too, eh? He was not too bad a sort. Just stupid. Maybe this will teach him not to work for crooks. Thanks for calling."

He came back to the table, sighing with satisfaction. The owner of the truck had been fined five hundred dollars and the driver fifty.

"Five hundred dollars! A junk man?" Maureen asked.

"Oh, he was rich, don't worry. But I'd have rather seen him jailed."

"What I can't understand," Brendan said as his father sat down, "is why anybody would dump good race horses that way. Aren't they valuable? Why couldn't he just sell them?"

Tim broke off a piece of bread and put some of Marge's wild-grape jam on it. "A race horse, when it's old, is no more valuable than any other old nag. They were old, too old to race by far. This man Farro, they tell me, is a big dealer in scrap metals, car parts, and so forth. Buys anything, sells it at a nice profit. He knew somebody had these horses to sell.

From Maryland, they came originally. Then he heard of this factory, up in Danbury, that buys mares for experiments. They make some kind of serum. A chemical plant it is, and Farro heard they paid a pretty good price. So he bought the mares dirt-cheap. But then it turns out the factory has all the mares it can use for six months or more. After a while he got tired of feeding them—he hadn't figured on the cost of oats —and there it was, winter. He couldn't turn them out to graze, so . . ."

A pair of headlights, coming to a stop before the cottage, interrupted the story. Marge opened the door, and Mr. Holiday came in.

"Well, Tim, I hear you've been playing cops and robbers."

"We have our two stableboys to thank for catching the culprits," Tim said, smiling at the girls.

"Is that right?" Carter Holiday asked, turning to them. "You caught the men yourselves—you two girls?"

Maureen grinned. "No, Wendy did it. She set a trap."

Wendy began to laugh. "I didn't. Tim trapped him. He was caught like a rabbit in a trap." She and Maureen burst out laughing, choking and almost doubled over.

"They're tired silly," Marge explained. "They get that way, you know. Want a ride home, kids? I'll drive you if Brendan will do the dishes. How about it, Brendan?"

He groaned. "I guess I'll have to," he said with a smile.

CHAPTER SEVENTEEN

The Green Hunter

Once more it was show time. Once more the stableboys of Holiday Farm rode in the horse van. Once more they waited while babies of five and six bounced through the Lead Line class, small backs almost covered by number placards, little velvet caps held on by chin elastics.

Once more Wendy and Maureen walked horses between classes and then scrambled to the fence to watch Tim take the high jumps of the outside course. It was a horse show like others—but with a difference.

For one thing, Barbara Holiday rode in Walk, Trot, and Canter, and won a red ribbon. For another, the girls showed King and Vogue as well as the ponies. But the most important difference of all was that Dan was entered in the Green Hunter class.

Tim did not know it, of course. The girls had hit upon the idea as a way of proving to people that Dan could behave and was worth buying.

They had talked it over with Brendan in the hayloft.

"I see your point," he said, "but who's going to tie the bell around the cat's neck?"

Wendy volunteered. "I will," she said. "I'll show Dan. I don't mind."

"No! Let me!" Maureen argued. "I'm stronger than you,

Wendy. I can manage that old smart aleck! Let him try to throw me. I'll—bite him!"

"Haw! Fat chance my father letting either of you near Dan." Brendan, scowling thoughtfully, picked up a piece of straw and broke it in two.

Maureen scooped up a handful of hay and sneaked up behind him, but Brendan caught her by the wrist. "Oh, no you don't!"

She transferred the straw to her other hand and tossed it at Wendy. Wendy threw it back, and Maureen tried to stuff another batch down her back. Wendy caught her around the knees, and they went rolling around the loft giggling.

"Cut it out," Brendan ordered. "I'm trying to think! Pipe down or I'll shove you both down the chute." He caught Wendy and held her over the opening.

"I give up! I give up!" She laughed, and both girls sat quietly, chins resting on their knees, until he spoke again.

"Okay. I've got it all worked out except for a minor detail." He grinned. "And that's just it: 'de tail.' Who's going to braid de tail?"

"My mother!" Wendy cried. "She watched Bert last time."

"She'll have to do it at the show grounds. And we don't need to van him, I can hack him up there. And I think Jerry will lend me the money for the entrance fee until I get paid. There's only one other thing: who'd work for me? I told them I'd work as jump boy again."

"Steven will. I'll ask my brother Steven," Wendy said, and Maureen was asking, "Why? What will *you* be doing?"

Brendan's mouth widened into a grin. "I'll be showing Dan."

And now the steward was announcing: *Entries for the Green Hunter Division, ready at the gate, please,* and the girls were running to watch. Boy and horse looked wonderful. Brendan's cheeks glowed healthily, and his blue eyes sparkled. Dan's coat gleamed. His tack shone, his hoofs had been oiled, and the tail that matched his reddish coat was braided almost as neatly as if Bert Buchanan had done it himself.

"My dad around?" Brendan whispered.

Tim was not there. He had just finished taking King over the outside course. But as the first of the green hunters entered the ring, he sauntered over with Bert and another groom. The girls ducked behind a car parked by the rail, and watched to see what would happen when Tim noticed Dan.

The third entry was in the ring. Tim glanced at it and turned to speak to Bert. Then his head swiveled around and his jaw dropped. "Holy hat! It's Brendan! On Dan! How the . . . ?"

Maureen and Wendy came from hiding to stand beside him, but Tim took no notice of them. His hands grasped the rail fence so tightly that his knuckles were white. "Bren-dan, come out of there, you fool!"

Marge came striding up. "Tim, did you know Brendan was going to . . ."

"Of course not! Do you think I'm crazy? *Brendan!*"

The boy only grinned at them as he took Dan around the ring.

Wendy was suddenly assailed with fears. What if Brendan were thrown as Tim had been? And Mr. Holiday had said that Tim was lucky, that a less capable rider would have been killed.

But Dan was behaving like a lamb. He took a small circle at an even trot and then broke into a canter. Brendan's eyes were on the jump ahead. He spoke encouragingly to the horse. The girls were stationed at the spot from which the other horses had taken off for the first jump, but Dan did not rise.

"Up! Get him up!" Tim shouted.

It looked as if Dan were going to run right into the fence. But suddenly Dan gave a strong thrust from hind feet that were well forward, folded his forelegs neatly, and was over.

Marge sighed. "Thank God."

"Sticky" was Tim's comment.

Wendy and Maureen tensed themselves for the second jump. Again the horse ran in close before taking the fence, and Tim pounded the rail in anger and swore under his breath. A shoe rang against the third fence.

"One tick," Bert Buchanan noted, "but that won't count necessarily." According to the program, ticks were not to count unless the fault of bad jumping.

"But that *was* a bad jump." Tim scowled. "And there's another," he said, as Dan took the last jump in the same manner as the others.

"What do you mean—bad?" Marge asked indignantly. "He came through it safely. What more do you want?" And they all ran to greet Brendan as he came out.

"Isn't that the horse that put you in the hospital, Tim?" someone asked.

"It is. And now you've seen him ridden by a mere lad. Is that your meaning?"

"Mere lad? He looks all of six feet. Could it be he's a better horseman?" The man was joking, and Brendan laughed at the idea.

"Better than Dad? That would take some going."

"Well!" Tim sighed. "You got through it safely, boy, but I must say he gave you a round of sticky jumps. Why didn't you get him to stand back?"

"Aw, he's all right, Dad. That's the way he likes to jump."

The steward's voice interrupted: *Line up, please.*

"I tried," Tim explained to Bert, as Brendan took Dan into

the ring and backed him into line with the other entries. "But if he jumps at all, that crazy roan, he runs close to the fence and pops over. I hate that kind of jumper."

"But he don't land stiff," another groom commented. "He lands nice and easy."

And then the announcement was coming over the loud-speaker. "*First, No. 23, Quicksilver, owned by the Connelly Stables; Second, Captain Dan, owned by Mr. and Mrs. Carter . . .*"

Tim's mouth fell open. The girls cheered wildly, and Bert thumped Tim on the back. "I guess the judges didn't think him a bad jumper."

"Who's judging this class?" Tim demanded. "He's crazy!" He strode toward the judges' tent.

"Hello, girls."

The girls looked up to find Colonel Kirby smiling at them. "Nice round Tim's boy had there."

They nodded in agreement, eager to get away and talk to Brendan.

"And I heard Captain Dan was dangerous, and that Holiday wanted to sell him. Isn't that the horse that gave Tim his concussion?"

"Yes, but Mr. Doyle wasn't feeling well that day," Wendy explained. "Dan's just a little spunky, isn't he, Maureen?"

"I hope you're right, because I want to make an offer for him. Is Carter Holiday here?"

Wendy nodded, and Maureen pointed to the black convertible parked near the judges' tent. As soon as he had gone, they whooped with joy. It had worked! Their plan had worked!

A moment later their smiles faded. Dan would be sold. They would not see him any more. The stable would not be the same. They suddenly looked at each other in panic. In another moment Dan would belong to a man whose groom beat horses!

They started after the Colonel, working their way through riders walking horses, through mounted riders, grooms, and owners talking in groups, and children in habits waiting for classes. They ran straight into Tim. He was arguing with the judge.

"In all my years of judging at horse shows," the small, wrinkled man was saying, "this is the first time anyone has ever complained over *getting* a ribbon."

"Sir, I'm not complaining," Tim explained. "I'm merely asking if you actually consider that good form and good jumping—or was it that the others were even worse?"

The little man looked up at Tim with wise eyes beneath white brows. "Mr. Doyle, in judging a hunter I consider only one thing: Will he give his rider a safe hunt? I cannot go by rumors, or by a horse's reputation. I go by what I see in the ring. He's not a showy jumper, the horse your son rode, but I wasn't judging him as an open jumper. If I had been, I would have given the red to that chestnut who went sky-high."

Maureen tugged at Tim's sleeve. They had to speak to him before the Colonel made an offer to Mr. Holiday for Dan. Just then the tinny voice of the loudspeaker announced the next class, No. 19. That was the Holiday Memorial, offered every year for riders under eighteen. The trophy, a bowl of sterling silver, twelve inches in diameter, had to be won three times to be kept. Several years ago Brendan had won it two years in a row, but it had been won last year and the year before by Donna Watts of Old Orchard Stables. Wendy was entered in this class on Vogue.

As she mounted, Tim ran up to check her stirrups. "All right, Wendy, we're depending on you. Remember, Donna

Watts has two legs on that trophy. If she wins it this time, it's hers."

A girl in a derby rode up on a gray.

"Is she only seventeen?" Wendy asked, staring at the mature-looking rider.

"Donna? Certainly she is! She's been seventeen for the last three years! But that's none of our business. Vogue can beat Sea Mist any day of the week."

Wendy agreed wholeheartedly. She rode down to the starting point to wait her turn. This event, Children's Hunters, took place on the outside course. She remembered how excited she and Maureen had felt at their first show, watching Tim take these same jumps on King. King had won the blue, and so should Vogue, if only she made no mistakes.

Wendy was not familiar with all of the horses entered, but Vogue ought to be able to beat Sea Mist. She had to!

The jump-boys lowered the fences to three-foot-six. There were eight to be taken. Donna Watts was the second to go. Applause. Sea Mist had gone well. Two other riders went over the course and then it was Wendy's turn.

She felt nervous. She and Maureen had practiced going over this course, but now, if she made one mistake, the Holidays would lose their chance of winning the trophy until next year. Worse, if Donna Watts came in first, they would lose it forever. It would go to the Watts' stable for keeps.

Wendy was tense. "We're depending on you," Tim had said. But she need not have worried. Sea Mist might be used to Donna, but Vogue was used to Tim. Compared to the six-foot-three groom, Wendy was weightless. Vogue soared over the eight fences as if carrying thistledown.

Three more entries followed. As Wendy waited for them to finish and then for the judges to confer, her thoughts went

back to Dan. She wondered if other stablemen had been as impressed with his round in the Green Hunter Division as had the Colonel. He and Mr. Holiday were together, talking. They might be settling Dan's fate at this very moment.

At last, the announcement. *First, number two.* Hurray! That was her number. Vogue had won the blue. The Memorial trophy was the Holidays', to keep! She leaned forward to pat Vogue. "Good girl! You did it!"

The O'Maras and the Masons and the Doyles were there to congratulate her.

"Good girl! The ribbons we've won today are past counting," said Tim. Then he shook his head. "But I still can't get over the judge giving the red to Dan. Not that I begrudge it to you," he said to Brendan, "even though you did make a fool of the old man."

"Go on, Tim." Mr. O'Mara laughed. "It didn't take Brendan to tell us you're getting old."

"Maybe I am," Tim acknowledged. "And maybe the boy is right—letting the horse go the way he wants. I've never believed in it."

"No! All you believe in is perfection!" said Marge. "In horses *and* people."

Marge held the trophy while Wendy dismounted. Then Wendy took the silver bowl and walked toward the black convertible.

"That's all right," Mr. Holiday insisted. "You won it; you keep it."

"Oh, no. It belongs to the stable. Brendan won it the other two times." Perhaps, though, Wendy thought, she would take it home just long enough to show everyone. But Mr. Holiday's generosity prompted her to ask a favor.

"Mr. Holiday, are you going to sell Dan to Colonel Kirby?"

He nodded. "He made me an offer. Not a very big one, only three hundred, but . . ."

"Three hundred! For a swell horse like Dan? Why, that's . . ."

"That's like giving him away," Mr. Holiday agreed. "But it's the only offer I've had. Isn't that what you asked me to do—sell him? I promised you I wouldn't have him shot, that I'd sell him if I could."

Wendy hung her head. Her face, reflected and distorted by the concave bowl, was fascinatingly ugly. Her eyes came together like pigs' eyes. Her chin was elongated, and her ears spread out. I'm pig-eyed, moose-faced, and jug-eared, she thought, and was reminded of something.

"Mr. Holiday," she blurted, "you don't want Dan in with

those roach-backed, goose-rumped, sickle-hocked, coon-footed excuses for horses that Colonel Kirby has in his stable!"

Carter Holiday roared. In imitating Tim's words she had unconsciously imitated his accent.

"Dan belongs in our stable with King and Vogue and the ponies!" she went on in a rush of words. "So why don't you give him to Tim? You said three hundred was like giving him away. Tim's always wanted a horse of his own, and Dan is the right horse for him, because Dan will always be a challenge. And Tim can hunt Dan, and your guests can hunt Vogue. And then if you want to, you can buy another horse for the empty stall." She stopped, breathless. She had never made such a long speech, not even in English class when called upon to do so.

"Dan's going to jump okay for Tim now," she said earnestly. "All he needs is a little gentling."

The big man smiled. "Tim, you mean?"

The luck of the Holiday horses held all day. Maureen won a blue in Ladies' Hunters on Lady, and King and Vogue ended as Champion and Reserve. In all, Tim had won so much prize money that he invited the girls to dinner at the Old Stone Mill. They drove off to the restaurant, ribbons pinned in masses to the right-hand sun visor of the car.

"You're to order a real dinner now," Tim told them when they were seated. "None of your 'I'll just have a hamburger' this time."

Maureen grinned defiantly over the menu. "All right for you! I'm going to order the de luxe dinner—complete!"

She ordered it. Oysters, clam chowder, roast beef, baked potato, peas, salad, and pie à la mode.

"Now let's see if she can eat it," Marge said.

She did, but it took a long time. Still, a long time was what they needed for post-mortems. Classes were reviewed, and horses and riders discussed. The plot to show Dan was confessed and forgiven. Mistakes were gone over. Winning rounds were repeated, jumps retaken, and moments when ribbons, prizes, and trophies were handed up were relived orally.

Tim summed up the day by saying, "Ah, well, we had good, sound, fair-minded judges for once, with brains in their craniums and eyes in their heads."

Maureen forced the last morsel of pie into her mouth and sank back.

Marge marveled at her. "I'll be darned! She did it!" And Tim regarded Maureen admiringly and said, "She gets more like her father every minute—in her figure, I mean."

Maureen grinned, but her eyes were heavy. Wendy, too, was tired. It had been a big day.

"We'd better get these jocks home before they disgrace us by falling asleep in their chairs," Tim observed.

"What about the—ooh'm—stable work?" they yawned.

"Brendan will help with what's necessary. The rest can wait till morning."

At Holiday Farm Tim and Brendan helped the girls gather up their clothes. Maureen threw hers in the back seat and fell in a heap on top of them. Wendy got in beside Marge, holding the silver bowl carefully in her lap.

The wheels grated on the gravel. Maureen was already asleep. As they passed the stable, Wendy sighed contentedly. The horses were in—all of them. The king, the queen, the prince, and princess—and the knave, Dan.

They turned down the drive. Wendy looked back at the cottage where she had bathed after her mud bath, where she had eaten so many meals, drunk so many cups of tea, and dressed for so many shows. Its lighted windows gave a friendly wink. Then they were out on the highway, where she and

Maureen had first seen Brendan and had taken him for a rich man's son.

The car windows were open. The evening air was soft and gentle. The ribbons on the visor fluttered silkily. Wendy's eyes closed, and she was riding Little Joe over a silvery moonlit field.

"Come on, boy, you can do it. Up!" she murmured as a stone wall five feet high rose before them. Then her head bobbed, her chin hit her chest, and she woke to find Marge regarding her with an indulgent smile.

"You can dismount now; you're home."